"You're More Beautiful Than Ever."

She knew his voice. Even if he had changed in appearance and manner, his voice was the same. For an instant she thought she would faint.

"Cade," she whispered. The man she had planned to marry was standing in front of her, close enough for her to touch. It was her first time seeing him in nine long years.

Everything in her screamed a protest. And deep down, most disturbing of all, was her response to him that she despised, yet could not control. Every nerve was raw; the beat of her heart was faster.

He stood holding out his hand to her. She moved automatically, going through motions without thinking about them, numb as she offered her hand. His warm hand enveloped hers in a surprisingly gentle shake, and the moment they touched she knew her life had changed.

Dear Reader,

A fascinating facet of life is a second chance. One of my favorite stories is Bernard Malamud's *The Natural* and the idea of a second chance in life. What happens when there is a second chance in love? *Scandals from the Third Bride* is the story of a woman jilted a week before her wedding when her fiancé vanishes from her life. Later, he calls and writes, but by that time, Katherine Ransome has been hurt too deeply to respond.

So, dear reader, here is the third member of the Ransome family, the younger sister, Katherine, and the story of the man who has entered her life for the second time. This gives them both another chance, so turn the page to see what Katherine and Cade do with their second chance for the passionate, intense love they once felt for each other.

Best wishes,

Sara Orwig

SARA ORWIG

SCANDALS FROM THE THIRD BRIDE

Published by Silhouette Books
America's Publisher of Contemporary Romance

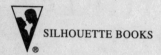 SILHOUETTE BOOKS

ISBN-13: 978-0-373-76762-5
ISBN-10: 0-373-76762-5

SCANDALS FROM THE THIRD BRIDE

Copyright © 2006 by Sara Orwig

Visit Silhouette Books at www.eHarlequin.com

Printed in U.S.A.

Recent books by Sara Orwig

Silhouette Desire

*Do You Take This Enemy? #1476
*The Rancher, the Baby &
 the Nanny #1486
Entangled with a Texan #1547
†Shut Up and Kiss Me #1581
†Standing Outside the Fire #1594
Estate Affair #1657
‡Pregnant with the First Heir #1752
‡Revenge of the Second Son #1757
‡Scandals from the Third Bride #1762

Silhouette Intimate Moments

*One Tough Cowboy #1192
†Bring on the Night #1298
†Don't Close Your Eyes #1316

*Stallion Pass
†Stallion Pass: Texas Knights
‡The Wealthy Ransomes

SARA ORWIG

lives in Oklahoma. She has a patient husband who will
take her on research trips anywhere, from big cities to
old forts. She is an avid collector of Western history
books. With a master's degree in English, Sara has
written historical romance, mainstream fiction and
contemporary romance. Books are beloved treasures
that take Sara to magical worlds, and she loves both
reading and writing them.

Special thanks to my editors,
Jessica Alvarez and Melissa Jeglinski.

One

After a short drumroll from the band, the emcee, Lance Wocek, stepped forward. "Here's our own beautiful Katherine Ransome," he announced, taking her hand, "talented artist, successful businesswoman and stunning bachelorette."

Smiling into the ring of bright spotlights on Fort Worth's Oak Hill Country Club's impromptu stage, Katherine waved to no one in particular. The patrons in tuxes and designer dresses made a ritzy gala of the elegant charity benefit for homeless children. Katherine was in sympathy with the cause, but she wished again that she had written a check instead of participating herself.

"Gentlemen, for an evening with the charming and beautiful Miss Ransome, what am I bid?" Lance asked. "Who'll start the bidding?"

"One thousand dollars," called a male voice and guests applauded. Trying to gaze beyond the lights, Katherine looked at a blur of faces turned in her direction, probably men she had known all her life.

"One thousand dollars! Good start! What am I bid?" Lance asked, circling and smiling at his audience.

"Two thousand," a man called, and she recognized local attorney Wes Trentwood's voice. She was glad men were bidding, remembering her brothers teasing her that no one would bid because she had been so cool in the past to the local males. So far, between the two bidders, she preferred an evening with Wes to anyone else.

"Two thousand dollars," Lance repeated. "We have a bid of two thousand dollars. Who'll make it three thousand for an evening with one of the most gorgeous ladies in the county?"

"Three thousand," came another bid that was raised immediately to four.

"I bid five hundred thousand dollars," a deep male voice said.

While an audible gasp rippled through the room, heads turned. Stunned that anyone would pay so much for an evening with her, Katherine peered in the direction of the voice.

As she watched, a man stood and applause broke out over his bid. He threaded his way between the tables of onlookers. Unable to distinguish his features because of the lights, Katherine could see his black hair and broad shoulders. He wasn't local, yet something about him struck a chord of familiarity. She could only stare in amazement, and then she reminded herself the money went to a good cause and his bid was a magnanimous donation.

As he approached the stage, even though she couldn't see him well because of the blinding lights, she discerned that he was tall and moved with the grace of a panther.

As he narrowed the distance between them, her heart thudded.

Katherine's pulse roared in her ears. Time hung suspended while she was flung back nine years. For an infinitesimal second, everything in her cried out to throw her arms around his neck and hug him. He stood as still as she, and the electricity jumping between them made her wonder why flames didn't scorch the air.

Her brain began to function, and the moment was gone. Longing vanished, replaced by surprise.

Dressed in a black tux and a snowy white shirt, he stopped in front of her and looked at her solemnly. "You're more beautiful than ever."

She knew his voice, knew the pitch and timbre, knew his brown eyes. Even if he had changed in appearance and manner, his voice was the same and sent tingles spiraling through her as if he had touched her.

Dismayed, she gazed at him while her head spun and her heart pounded, drowning out all noise. For an instant she thought she would faint.

"Cade," she whispered. Cade Logan, the man she had planned to marry was standing in front of her, close enough for her to touch. It was her first time to see him in nine long years, since the week before their wedding.

Lance spoke to Cade or to her. She had no idea which one. Someone called Lance's name and he excused himself, leaving without either one of them answering him.

She was held in a gaze that shut off the rest of the world. Nine years ago and suddenly, here Cade was standing before her. She had thought about this occasion over and over again, and played multiple versions of it in her mind. Now that it was actually happening, she was unprepared, and the moment wasn't like anything she had rehearsed in her fantasies.

Everything in her screamed a protest. And deep down, most disturbing of all, her first thought was, he was too handsome for words. She had a response to him that she despised, yet could not control. Her reaction rocked her because she had thought she was over him long ago and immune to ever seeing him again. There was nothing resistant in her system. Every nerve was raw; the beat of her heart was faster.

He stood holding out his hand to her. She moved automatically, going through the motions without thinking about them, numb as she offered her hand. His warm hand enveloped hers in a surprisingly gentle shake, and the moment they touched, an electric jolt went to her toes.

She yanked her hand away and narrowed her eyes, while her anger surfaced and overrode other emotions.

Rage, pure and deep, shook Katherine, sending tremors through her body. She wanted to wave her fists and shout at Cade, to scream at him and pound on his chest. Instead, she lifted her chin and gazed away coolly in disdain as if she hadn't even recognized him.

"This is Friday night. As I understand it, I've acquired the privilege of taking you to dinner tomorrow night," Cade said. She ached to decline. But she had made a commitment and little kids were depending on her.

"How dare you! How can you show up here like this?" she hissed between clenched teeth unable to hold back, yet aware they still stood spotlighted on stage. Her fists doubled and she shook. "You can't possibly expect me to go out with you, of all people."

"I not only expect it, I just paid a hell of a lot of money for the evening with you," he answered quietly, thoroughly scrutinizing her, which only heightened her fury.

"There are several others you can take to dinner tomorrow night who will be much more receptive. Perhaps you'd rather go with someone else."

"No, Katherine. I knew what I was doing when I bid for an evening with you," he answered with a note of steel in his voice. Beneath her anger was a dim awareness that he was far more self-assured and confident than he had been nine years ago. He had to be worth a royal fortune to have tossed away five hundred thousand dollars to go out for a few hours with her. Occasionally, she had read about him in newspapers or seen articles or pictures in magazines and she knew he was a successful business entrepreneur, but she hadn't dreamed the extent of his fortune. How had he made so much money in such a short time? Why was he back? Questions buzzed in her head.

Lance returned and his voice finally penetrated her shock. Lance extended his hand toward Cade and they shook hands.

"Thank you, sir, for your overwhelming donation to this fine cause. Your generosity will be deeply appreciated for years to come. You'll change many children's lives. And in return, you get an evening out with one of Fort Worth's most beautiful women, Katherine Ransome.

"Before we go any further, let me introduce myself. I'm Lance Wocek. We're overwhelmed by your donation that's the largest we've ever had in any local charity event from a single donor that I recall." He looked expectantly at Cade.

"Lance, you two know each other," Katherine interjected in a tight voice. The two men had grown up in Cedar County and gone through Rincon High School together and she had been four years behind them. "Remember Cade Logan?" she asked. "Cade, I'm sure you recall Lance."

Lance's jaw dropped, and his eyes grew round while he stared at Cade. "Cade Logan? From high school? You've changed," he stammered. "I didn't recognize you," Lance said as if talking to himself, and Katherine remembered the wild, slender boy who had won her love.

She could clearly see his shaggy long hair, tattered T-shirts and faded jeans and she had to concede that he did look different. She herself hadn't recognized him at first. She surveyed the differences, noticing he had filled out his lanky six-foot-four-inch frame with broad shoulders. His black hair was neatly trimmed and combed. There was a subtle difference in his demeanor, a presence about him that indicated a "take charge" personality that hadn't been there before.

But the sexy bedroom eyes with thick lashes were the same. He could still flash the penetrating look that always made her feel as if he knew her every thought. His full, sensual lower lip was the same, as was his wide, sculpted mouth.

"I'm the same Cade Logan," Cade said easily. "It's been a while."

"None of us—" Suddenly Lance broke off and looked back and forth between Katherine and Cade. "You two…" His voice trailed away, and he looked stricken.

"I'll make arrangements with Katherine for our evening together," Cade said smoothly. "I have a check here for the five hundred thousand. Shall I make it out to the Slade House Children's Foundation?" Cade asked, pulling out his checkbook and pen.

"That'll be fine," Lance said, staring at Cade until someone spoke to him and he had to turn away again.

Katherine couldn't believe what was happening. She hoped it was a nightmare that would vanish upon waking.

Only it wasn't disappearing. Cade gazed at her with unfathomable brown eyes, and she didn't have any idea what was running through his mind.

"Why are you doing this? You can't possibly want to go out with me."

"I think I've shown that I do want to go out with you. I want to see you and this was the quickest, simplest way to do so."

"It was rather costly."

"I didn't want to hassle over you with someone, nor did I want you to back out of the evening. It's far more difficult to change your mind and your promise when so much is at stake for the kids."

"Your donation will be wonderful for the charity."

"I was happy to help that cause. Where should I pick you up and how is six?"

"Six is way too early," she said, hoping she could go late and come home early. You can pick me up at this address," she said, opening a small, black bag and producing one of her business cards. She turned it over, retrieved a pen and scribbled her address before handing the card to him. Again his fingers brushed hers and sent another electrifying jolt to her system.

He glanced at it, looking from it to her in a curious scrutiny that made her want to fidget and ask him what he was thinking.

Instead, she gazed coolly back at him and hoped he couldn't detect her racing pulse or ragged breathing or any other reaction she was having to seeing him. Why was he here? The big question had always been why had he left, but now, the answer to why he had returned was more pressing.

"Have you had dinner tonight?" he asked.

"No, I haven't, but if we go out tonight, that's the night you just bid for and won."

"That's fair enough," he said. "Can you leave now?"

"Leave? They'll serve a very elegant dinner here. That's part of the evening. Then there's dancing afterward," she said, unable to think about dancing with him and being in his arms again.

"I'd rather get out of here where we can be to ourselves. I don't care to be interrupted all evening. Is there any arrangement that as a participant you have to stay?"

"No, not at all. My part in the auction is over. I'll tell them I'm leaving and join you at the door," she said, both relieved they would get the evening together over quickly and on edge about going out with him.

If she ever saw him again, she had always expected that she would hate him, but that wasn't what she felt. Fury was dominant, but she responded to him as a female would to a sexy, appealing male. The evening alone with him made her tingly and excited even though she didn't want it to.

After telling a coordinator she was leaving, Katherine hurried to one of the private rooms that the bachelorettes had been given to use as a dressing room. She paused to look at herself in the mirror, glancing swiftly over her sequined sleeveless black dress with a low-cut vee neckline. She wore high-heeled black pumps.

Taking a deep breath, she left, hurrying toward the exit and experiencing another jolt when her gaze met Cade's as he watched her approach. A few hours with him and the evening would be over, she reminded herself. She could guard her heart and emotions for that long, surely.

He held the door open for her and then walked beside her, sliding his arm around her waist while they stepped outside into a cool October night. She felt the light contact with Cade as if it were a burning brand. She was prickly with raw awareness of his shoulder against hers, his arm circling her waist and her hip lightly touching his.

In the front of the club at the porte cochere, a limousine waited with a driver, who opened the door for her. Cade climbed in and sat beside her, turning slightly to face her.

Gazing back at him, she almost felt as if she were with a stranger. She didn't know Cade any longer. There was only a dim connection to the boy he once was and the person she knew. Yet there was no way to wipe out memories or her hurt or her anger.

"Why are you here?" she asked bluntly.

"Reasonable question. Some curiosity about you and my past. But that part is minor."

"So what's the big reason?" she persisted.

"I've found that ninety-nine percent of the time, when you purchase something, it's worth the difference to get the best."

"So you're here in Fort Worth to get the best of whatever it is you want."

"That's right. Why were you in the bachelorette auction?"

"The Slade Home is one of my favorite projects. Little children shouldn't be on the streets. You helped the children enormously tonight," she said, aware that he deserved thanks for what he had done for the kids.

"But, at the same time, you'd rather I hadn't bid."

"No. The money is more important and it'll do many needed things," she said, thinking how bland their conversation was while sparks ignited the air between them, and she fought the attraction for him that pulled at her as if he had never walked out and the past hadn't been filled with hurt.

"You could have written a check to the charity, so I'll inquire again, why did you participate?" he persisted.

"I've been asking myself that all evening," she remarked dryly, still having the feeling of talking to a stranger, except for his voice. She knew his voice. Even his hands were different—larger, less roughened.

"So the men who bid didn't particularly mean anything to you?"

"Not at all. I recognized one man and we're friends. Where do you live?" she asked, curious in spite of wanting to ignore Cade.

"I live most of the year in Los Angeles, part of the time in Pebble Beach, part of the time in Switzerland. I'm building a house in Houston."

"You've done well. Sometimes I've read about you," she said. "According to the papers, you're an entrepreneur involved in investments and finance," she said, leaving out that every time she had read about him, she had wondered how someone who had been penniless and a high school dropout— a mechanic whose expertise had been bikes and cars—could have investments, but she didn't want to give him the satisfaction of asking about his life.

"Katie," he said, reverting back to the name he had always called her.

"It's Katherine," she snapped. "I don't care to be called Katie by anyone."

"Very well, Katherine," he said in a flat tone of voice that gave no indication of what he really felt.

There was no wedding ring on his finger, nor would there have been if he'd bid for her time for an evening. Cade had been wild, the local bad boy. Friends had warned her he would never settle and he wouldn't go through with the wedding. And they had been correct in their dire predictions.

"You've done well," he remarked.

"I enjoy my work," she said, wondering how he knew anything about her business. She became silently aware they were in downtown Fort Worth now. She gazed at the tall building that held Ransome Design, Incorporated. She had two floors and sixty employees and she dreamed of opening more offices. Her company was growing fast and she usually experienced a rush of pleasure on viewing the building with her office, but her emotions churned over Cade, and she didn't feel the customary satisfaction. Thanks partially to the man seated facing her, her work was her life.

She turned to find him watching her.

"A penny for your thoughts," he said quietly. "As the old saying goes."

"It won't cost you even a cent. I was looking at the building where I have my business."

"Ransome Design, Incorporated had a very impressive twenty percent growth over a year ago. You've made a name for yourself, too."

"My job is my whole life," she said. "I suspect you can understand that."

He shrugged one shoulder casually. "There are other things more important," he said, his dark gaze boring into her.

"Not in my life," she answered and turned away to look out the window again. She could feel his gaze remaining on her and she wished she could lose the prickly awareness of him, the attraction that made him larger-than-life in too many ways.

She had no inclination to engage in conversation with Cade. She stayed on a raw edge, hanging on to her temper and all the accusations she had accumulated over time.

She wondered what was going through his mind, because he was quiet and didn't try to engage her in any polite conversation, which would have been pointless.

She didn't want to be alone with him. She didn't want to be with him, period. In her peripheral vision, she could see him, and while she tried to ignore him, it was impossible. His long legs were stretched out near hers.

In minutes they stopped in front of another tall building and she realized their destination was the exclusive and prestigious Millington Club on the twenty-sixth floor. Her father belonged to the Millington, as well as the Petroleum Club, and she was surprised Cade even knew about it. She was certain he had known nothing about the exclusive clubs when he was growing up in Rincon in Cedar County, Texas.

They rode the elevator and emerged at a reception area with a thick navy carpet and mahogany furniture. To her surprise, she realized Cade had reservations. She watched while he talked to the maitre d'. As the two men conversed briefly, her gaze ran down the length of Cade, and she remembered exactly how it felt to be in his arms, pressed against that strong, hard body, his legs tangled with hers. Heat coiled low inside her and she clenched her fists, trying to ignore feelings and banish memories and desire.

He wore a simple watch with a leather band, but in the limo she had seen his watch was one of the most expensive brands. She suspected he'd meant what he'd said about having the best. And who was the woman in his life now? Cade wouldn't be without one.

When he turned to take her arm, his hand touching her was as electrifying as any other contact they had had tonight. Trying to ignore everything about him and continually failing,

Katherine walked beside him as they were shown to a linen-covered table beside floor-to-ceiling windows that overlooked the bright city lights. Soft piano music played and couples already were on the dance floor. She gazed across the table into Cade's dark eyes.

"As I recall you like prime rib and they serve it here," he said, and she drew a deep breath. Pain and fury and surprise mixed in her that he would remember. "We weren't into drinking wine, so I don't know your preference there," he said.

"My tastes have changed and tonight, I think I'll start with a cup of black coffee," Katherine said, intending to keep as clear a head as possible around Cade. She saw a flare of amusement in his dark eyes as he ordered white wine for himself.

"You're an entrepreneur, so what's your latest project?" she asked, not caring, just wanting to get to an impersonal topic.

"I just acquired a film company. The news became public yesterday."

She remembered seeing an article in the paper that she had merely glanced at without making the connection to Cade. She did remember it was one of the oldest and one of the last still family-owned. "I saw that the studio sold," she admitted, "but I didn't take the time to read about who had bought the business. I didn't think about it being you. You're going into show business—are you seeing an actress?"

"No. It was good investment and the company was on shaky footing and about to go under. As far as an actress is concerned, at the moment there's no woman in my life."

"I find that difficult to imagine," she remarked dryly and he smiled, a smile that took her breath and hurt. Creases bracketed his mouth and memories tore at her. To escape from her tormenting thoughts, she picked up a thick black folder and opened it to study the menu.

"It's true, there's nobody," he commented. "Who's the man in your life, Katherine?"

"There isn't one. I wouldn't have been in the bachelorette auction if there was anyone on a serious basis. There isn't even anyone on a not-so-serious basis. I spend most of my time involved in my work."

"Then we're alike there," he said. "I could have given you the same answer. So there's no particular man in your life right now and no woman in mine."

"Don't make anything of that," she said sharply. "For me, it means nothing. And it doesn't matter."

His gaze caught and held hers in another penetrating look that made her wonder what he was thinking. Could he feel her rage? If he did, it didn't disturb him, but then, why should it? He hadn't cared when he had walked out on her without a word only a week before their wedding.

"I can't believe you would come back to Texas. When I look at you, Cade, all I feel is hurt and anger and hate!" she admitted, the words pouring out, yet an inner voice screamed she felt something else, too. Attraction was hot, volatile, impossible to ignore.

She became silent when the sommelier came to the table to open wine for Cade and let him approve the selection. While Cade's wine was being poured, a waiter came to pour her steaming black coffee and ice water for both Cade and her.

Once they were alone again, Cade raised his wineglass. "Here's to our efforts tonight to help children." His dark eyes were riveting and held her, fanning her desire. It was an effort to tear her gaze from him.

"I'll drink to that," she said, picking up her water and reaching out to touch Cade's goblet lightly. His hand touched hers and he watched her as they sipped.

"How civilized we're being," she said in a tight voice, grinding out the words and unable to contain her fury. "All I want to do is shout and scream at you."

"I can understand. We hurt each other, Katherine," he said solemnly.

"Then why did you come back here to open it all up?" she asked, wondering again where *each other* came in and how she could possibly have hurt him? She couldn't guess how he had twisted the past in his mind because there was no earthly way she had done anything at the time to cause him pain and she wanted to fling that fact right back at him, but she clamped her mouth shut.

"The past is far behind us and we've both moved on," he said. "I expected to find you married with a family."

"I'm married to my work," she remarked. "You gave me a convoluted answer when I asked why you're here and why you wanted an evening with me. What's the real reason?"

Two

"I've seen some of the work you've done. It's fabulous," Cade said. "I have a project I want to discuss. I hope to hire you."

She gazed at him coolly. "I won't work for you, Cade. How dare you waltz in and expect to hire me!"

"I could have sent someone with a corporation name you'd never have recognized. You would have taken the job. As a matter of fact, until a few days ago, that's what I intended to do. At first, I thought it would be best if our paths never crossed. I wasn't any more eager to see you than you have been to see me."

"So what made you change your mind?"

"I realized that as soon as you learned who owned the house, you might have walked out. Of course, I could have kept you from ever knowing. I have companies that you'd have to investigate to know that I own them, and I doubt if you check on all your clients."

"No. I've never seen any need to do so."

"I considered the possibility of staying out of it and keeping you from knowing, but later, it would come up sometime that there's a house in Houston with your murals and a reporter would dig through the facts to find out who the homeowner is. Also, if I'm here, I can make sure I get what I want."

"So you chose to come yourself. You want to hire my company's services. Cade, I'm not for hire where you're concerned. Get another ad agency. The world is filled with them."

"They don't all paint house murals and I don't want your agency. It's you I want to hire."

"No! I won't work for you."

"I've been told by people in Houston, Chicago and L.A., that you're the best in the country at painting murals, interior or exterior."

"That's good to hear," she said, not really caring at the moment what he'd learned about her company or her. Why did he have to come back so damned handsome and so self-assured?

"I've heard that from people who had no idea where I grew up or that I knew you. You're recommended by gallery people, museums and your former customers. I've seen your work and it's top-notch. I told you, I prefer the best."

"That's flattering, but there are others who are skilled at their craft and they can create scenes that will be as artistic as any I paint," she replied, certain that there was no way he could talk her into working for him.

"I've heard differently."

"I promise you, there are others who can paint as well. Graham Trevor is one. He's excellent, and there are plenty of examples of his work for you to view. A mural is a simple thing to do."

"Right, Katherine, if you're good at doing them. Otherwise, it's a difficult challenge." Cade leaned back in his chair with one hand on his hip. "I don't want Graham Trevor or anyone else except you. Surely we can both get past what happened nine years ago."

"No, I can't! I don't want to. I hate you for what you did and I don't want to work with you now. How plain do I have to say it?" she cried. She hurt and he was opening old wounds. Worst of all, right now in the midst of all their bickering, she wanted his arms around her.

"I figured by now that you would have let go of the past. It's been over a long time," he said and his words cut like a knife. How could he dismiss the past so easily when it had hurt so badly? But maybe it hadn't hurt him at all, she reminded herself.

"I'm sure it's forgotten for you. Obviously, it was over for you before you left Texas nine years ago."

"We don't have to be together for you to accept me as your client. I'll pay you well."

"I'm sure you would, but I don't want your money, your business or anything to do with you," she said, absolutely certain that there weren't any circumstances in which she would agree to work for him.

They halted their discussion because the waiter came to take their dinner order. Even though she preferred prime rib, she didn't want to give Cade the satisfaction of thinking she was the same person as she used to be. "I'll have the pecan-crusted trout," she said and the waiter nodded. She glanced at Cade to see a questioning expression as he ordered lobster. As soon as the waiter left, Cade leaned forward.

"So prime rib is no longer first choice with you?"

"No. Most all of my choices have changed through the years."

He stared at her with a look of speculation. "There's no reason to argue all evening. Let's settle this right now." While he continued to watch her, he took out a cellular phone and spoke so quietly, she could barely hear him. He put away the phone and stood, coming around to hold her chair.

"Let me show you something," he said, and her curiosity was stirred because she couldn't imagine what he intended. Walking close beside her, he took her arm. Before they left the restaurant, Cade paused to tell the maitre d' to delay their dinners until they returned. Her curiosity grew over where they were going. They left the building and crossed the street to one of Fort Worth's best hotels.

"I have a room here. That's why we're eating at the Millington Club instead of the Petroleum Club tonight. The Millington is closer. I want to show you something that I intended to show you after dinner."

She balked and stopped walking. "Your hotel room?"

"That's where we're going. I have blueprints of the home I'm building. It won't hurt you to come up and look and then we'll go right back for dinner."

"I don't need to see any blueprints," she insisted. "We have nothing to discuss."

"Yes, we do. I want to talk to you about murals for my house."

"There isn't enough money in the world for you to hire me to paint for you," she said, facing him and touching his chest with her index finger. "No, Cade." Seething, she burned and perspiration dotted her forehead. She wanted away from him. At any moment she was afraid she would lose the iron control she was exercising and let fly all the accusations she had stored up for nine long years. And that last day was as fresh in her mind as if it had happened yesterday. To her surprise, Cade's appearance had brought back the monumental hurt when she had thought she had finally been free of it.

"There might be a price that you'd agree to," he answered quietly. "I have blueprints. At least look at what I want."

"No!" she cried. "There's no point in it. None! I'm not working for you and opening up old wounds or causing myself anguish. You've hurt me enough, dammit!"

"'Dammit' is right," he charged in a low voice. "This is

work, not our private lives. It's just that everyone—I mean all the galleries and the ad people and the artists—says that you're the best. Start being the professional that I know you are," he ordered. "We have the rest of the evening and nothing to do except eat or shout at each other about past hurts or discuss the paintings I intend to have in my new house. Come look at my blueprints." He tugged lightly on her arm. "You're the expert. Come look."

Reluctantly, she nodded and got another warm smile. As they crossed the lobby, he stopped at the desk to pick up a large roll of papers.

In silence they took the elevator to a suite on the top floor of the hotel. Cade unlocked the door and held it open for her.

She entered a large living area with beige and white decor. An adjoining dining area held a table with chairs for eight. Through open doors she could see two bedrooms and beyond sliding glass doors was a balcony with an iron table and chairs.

Cade shed his coat, and she remembered times he had taken off his coat before turning to make love to her. Her mouth went dry as he slipped out of the coat and draped it over a chair. When she had known him before he had been fit, muscled and strong. She guessed that hadn't changed.

As she watched, Cade cleared a crystal vase of fresh flowers off the dining table and she joined him while he opened the blueprints. No way did she want to work for him or even have someone else in her firm hired by him. She was conscious he stood only a couple of feet away. She looked at his well-shaped hands as he smoothed out the stiff paper. He had become far more appealing, but she supposed she saw some of the same things in him now that she had when they had been younger and madly in love.

In another reminder of how successful he had become, she looked down at the prints that held a drawing of a Greek Revival mansion that had two immense wings and was three stories tall. Surprised, she glanced into his dark eyes that as so often before, caught and held her, making her forget what she had intended to say. His dark eyebrows arched questioningly.

"What is it, Katherine?" he asked.

She didn't want to admit that she had lost her train of thought. "You left here without funds. You've done well, Cade."

"I've been lucky," he said in an offhand manner as if he hadn't done anything more than the next person. "Here's my house. It's under construction and I'm not living there now. I want murals in six of the rooms."

"Cade, this is such a waste of time," she said in exasperation. She couldn't imagine working for him because she was having difficulty getting through an evening with him.

"Give me a price," he urged, facing her. His calmness and persistence were wearing her patience thin.

"No, I won't. Don't you realize that I absolutely have hated you for walking out on our wedding? Do you have any idea how that hurt?" she asked, shaking as she let go some of her restraint. His patient silence irritated her even further.

"You humiliated me and broke my heart!" she cried out. "I was devastated. I didn't imagine anything could hurt like I did!" she exclaimed. The words came tumbling out and now that she'd started, she couldn't stop. "You didn't give me one reason why, or one scrap of a warning. You were gone. Running out on me in the worst, cruelest possible way."

He flinched and paled beneath his tan, but he had an inscrutable expression that hid his feelings.

Suddenly she let go, all the pent-up fury boiling to the surface, and she reached out to slap him.

Like lightning he caught her wrist and held her firmly, but not tightly enough to hurt her. "You're not going to strike me when you don't know why or what occurred back then," he said.

They were both breathing hard, tension drawn tightly between them while he held her wrist. Rage consumed her.

Fire flashed in his dark eyes and the clash between them was tangible. While they stared at each other, he clamped his jaw tightly shut as if holding back harsh words, which was exactly what she was trying to do. The moment drew out and then, as they stared at each other, her anger changed.

While she gazed into depths of brown, he looked at her mouth. When he did, her lips tingled. From the very first his kisses always melted her and erased any resistance to him.

Desire flamed, building heat inside her. They both were breathing hard. For an instant, everything else fell away except hunger for his kiss. She almost leaned toward him, started to and then realized what she was doing. She yanked her head back and shook her shoulders.

"Damn you, Cade. And you're still not going to explain why you walked out."

"I didn't come back to Texas to dredge up old hurts and fling accusations. That's over," he said, releasing her wrist. "I'm not going there because we could hurt each other more than ever. There's no point in stirring up resentment over the past. Not now. You were hurt at the time and for that I'm sorry," he said with a dismissal that added to her fury. Yet even as his voice remained calm, she could feel the tension stretching and fiery sparks flying between them, invisible, yet tangible.

"Sorry is so completely inadequate!" she cried, jerking her arm free and spinning away from him to walk to the window again. Tears threatened, and she fought to get a grip because she didn't intend to shed one tear over him. Not after all this time and all the control she had achieved. Where was all that restraint she had maintained through the years?

She wrapped her arms around her middle and hugged herself. "I don't want to have anything to do with you, Cade," she said.

"You can look at my house plans for a minute. There's no commitment in looking. Come back over here, Katherine."

She turned to glare at him and he stood, impassively

waiting until it seemed ridiculous and childish to refuse to look at his blueprints. She crossed the room to stand a few feet away from him.

As she gazed at the drawing of the house, she was again amazed by his success, which was greater than the news articles or the magazines had indicated.

"This is the dinning room and I want a mural on this wall," he said, pointing with his index finger. "One of the other walls will have mullioned windows that will prevent a clear view of the outside, so I want a landscape."

She examined a drawing of a room with a cathedral ceiling and an enormous stone fireplace that had a medieval flair, and she could imagine a scene of a European countryside on one wall. He wanted six murals. Her usual price popped into mind and she suspected that she could easily get more from Cade. She tried to stifle any thoughts about the income and what she could do with it for her company. What a windfall the job would be if it had been anyone else who wanted to hire her!

Cade shifted papers and she watched his well-shaped hands as he carefully smoothed a print. She could remember those hands on her body, moving over her seductively, magic hands that had set her aflame. Everything he did provoked memories that were too vivid. Attempting to focus totally on his plans, she leaned over the table to peer at the drawings. Cade moved closer beside her and turned over a page to look at the next drawing. "Here's the kitchen and dining area and I want a painting in here."

"Why are you showing me these pictures? The answer is no," she repeated, wondering if he ever heard "no" any longer.

"You're letting your emotions rule your judgment because you're turning down good business. My house will get attention and it would be advertising for you," he said, turning to study her. He stood only a couple of feet from her and she drew a deep breath. Why couldn't she handle being near him?

When she was so angry with him, she hated to discover that she was still incredibly attracted to him.

"This is one time I don't want the business," she said, wishing her racing pulse would slow.

"Let me show you the other rooms," he said, shifting pages around. He leaned over the table to point with his finger. "I want a mural on this wall. You can select the subject. Of course, I have to approve what you propose before you do it."

"You don't trust me, either."

"Yes, I trust you. I want to see what you have in mind. I'm the one who'll have to live with it. Give me a price, Katherine," he said softly. "You have to be enough of a business-woman and professional to look at what I have and give me a bid. Don't say no over old hurts. There is surely some point where it would become worth your while."

As he stared at her, their clash of wills was offset by her attraction, and she guessed he felt it, too. "No, there isn't because I don't want to work for you in any manner," she said tightly and turned to walk away. For one fleeting second she was tempted to fling some impossible price at him, like five hundred thousand per mural, and see if he would back down. The money was a temptation because she was ambitious, but she put the possibility out of mind.

She walked to the balcony door, opened it and stepped outside without allowing herself to think about what the job would mean to her. A cold gust of wind whipped around her and she wrapped her arms around her middle.

"All right," he said. She turned to find him standing in the doorway, leaning one shoulder against the jamb as he faced her. "I'll make you an offer."

She shook her head. "There's no point in it."

"I've told you that I want six murals. How's eight million dollars for all of them?"

She lost her breath as if she had received a blow. Stunned,

she stared at him. "Eight million dollars?" she gasped over the amount. She couldn't imagine such extravagance.

"That's too much!" The words were out before she thought.

"No, the price isn't too high if I get what I want," he replied smoothly. "I'll pay all your expenses, of course."

Again, he had shocked her profoundly. Never had she commanded such a price for her paintings. Her head spun over the amount and what she could do with it.

"You surely can use the income for something," he remarked dryly.

"Yes, I can," she said, barely able to get out the words. "Cade, I can't believe you'd pay so much to get my art. You can hire perfectly good painters who will do a fine job for you for vastly less."

"Maybe I owe you, Katherine," he said quietly.

"A payoff," she snapped, her temper rising, but there was no way to get the amount that he had offered her out of mind. Her plans for the future of her advertising company flashed, impossible to ignore. His murals would enable her to do what she wanted years sooner than she had expected. "Eight million for six murals," she repeated as if she couldn't believe what she'd heard.

He crossed the balcony to her and placed his hands on her shoulders.

Even though her pulse jumped, she shook her head at him. "No, no. You're not buying my body with that offer."

"I'm only standing here with my hands on your shoulders," he replied in a husky voice that made her forget the money and the murals and everything except Cade. Wind blew locks of his black hair and she remembered how it felt to run her hands through his hair. His hands were warm and he ran them up and down her upper arms, sliding his fingers slowly, lightly in a provocative touch.

"You're more beautiful than ever," he whispered.

"Stop, Cade. We're not going back there," she said, but her heart thudded and she trembled, aching for him as if it were yesterday when she had last seen him.

He ran his finger across her lower lip. "Beautiful, Katherine."

Tingles spiraled from his touch and her lips parted. The moment she realized her reaction, she twisted away to walk around him. "Let's go inside."

He followed her in and closed the door. "You know you can take the money, invest it and retire."

"Never!" she exclaimed, frowning at him as he joined her at the table again. "My work is my life. I thrive on painting and would never consider quitting."

He tilted his head to one side. "I know you took art classes, but I don't recall that you had any burning ambition."

"I threw myself into work to get over being hurt when you left, and then I discovered that I like success. All my life I've competed with my brothers. I want to make more money than they do, and now I might be able to do so."

"You'll have to go some to top your brother Nick. If you accept my offer, you might pass Matt."

She studied the drawings spread in front of her.

"Here they are," he said, leaning slightly over the table to spread more drawings out. "Here's each room that I'd like to have murals in. I don't have any idea what to put in these rooms. It's up to you to select the picture."

"I usually furnish the ideas about three quarters of the time," she said. "Occasionally, someone knows exactly what he wants," she answered without thinking about what she was saying to him. The amount of money dazed her. She turned to him. "You can afford to toss out eight million to get these murals?"

"Yes, I can. I've been fortunate."

She had been adamant that she wouldn't work for him, but his offer was impossible to refuse. She would be certifiable if she turned him down. She could do his murals without succumbing to his charm, she promised herself. And she knew there would be charm. He had melted her heart before when he had been rough and a boy and without means. Now he would be irresistible.

She moved along the table, spreading papers and looking at precise line drawings of floor plans, but she was doing it merely as an excuse to buy time while she mulled over his offer. Could she do the murals and resist Cade at the same time? Maybe he would go back to California or wherever he worked most of the time. As swiftly as she thought about it, she dismissed it. No matter what he said, she knew he would oversee the project.

Eight million dollars for his murals. The offer was temptation with no way to refuse. Yet she could not keep from wondering how badly he wanted her. Curiosity tempted her. With her heart pounding, she looked up at him, wondering if she dared raise the amount. If he refused, she would back down instantly. "I'll do your six murals for ten million," she offered.

Holding her breath and frightened by her own audacity, she saw amusement flash in the depths of his dark eyes, which surprised her. She had expected almost any other kind of reaction from him. "A few minutes ago you told me that I proposed too much."

"I was in shock over your offer. Now, I'm thinking about business."

"Then we've got a deal," he said, and she let out her breath. "Ten million it is."

Ten million! Her reputation would be instantly established by the price. Soon, she could do the ambitious projects she had only dreamed about before.

"How do you want payment?" he asked. "How's half now and half when you finish?"

She inhaled deeply. "You're one surprise after another," she admitted. "Why would you pay so much up front?"

"I'm certain you'll deliver, so why not? You can put the

cash to use right away. I can write you a check now for the first half, or Monday morning we can go to a bank and have the funds transferred to your account."

"Let's go to the bank Monday morning," she said, unable to believe such a thing was actually happening.

"Let me show you the rest," he said, stepping close beside her and pointing to blue lines on another page. "This is a recreation room. It'll have a pool table. This is an interior room, so I want something in here, too, that will bring in the outdoors. I want the mural along this wall," he said, drawing his finger in a line across the blueprint. "Something festive."

"I'll give you several choices and if you don't like any of them, I'll do more."

"Fair enough," he said and she realized she would be working with him constantly until he approved the murals she would paint.

"Then this room," he said, reaching for another sheet and brushing against her arm as he pulled the blueprint in front of them. "This is an exercise room. Do something to liven it up. Something cheerful. Nothing is more monotonous than a treadmill, so give me a picture along this wall that I can enjoy viewing."

She knew she would have to give thought and planning to what she would paint. She couldn't make any suggestions at this point and she was certain he didn't expect her to.

"Then over here," he said, reaching beyond her and brushing against her again. Catching a whiff of his aftershave, she could see the faint dark stubble of his beard that was beginning to show as he leaned forward, close in front of her. Did he even notice when they touched each other? Was he doing it deliberately or without thought? She couldn't keep from noticing and tingling as if the contact had been a caress.

"There's no woman who should have a say in this?"

Katherine asked, wishing she could take back the personal question the moment it was out.

He straightened and focused intently on her. "I told you before that there isn't a woman. The only person who has a say in this is me." He rested his hand on her shoulder again, but this time, he rubbed it slightly, touching a lock of her hair. "But as long as you brought it up—"

"Cade, I'm taking this job when I never intended to, but I want us to leave the past out of it. I don't want to go into personal things. Let's work as if we were two strangers who met tonight for the first time."

"If I'd met you tonight for the first time, I'd be flirting with you every minute of the evening," he said solemnly, his gaze drifting lazily over her features. His fingers trailed along her jaw.

Ignoring him, she turned back to the blueprints. "All right, we've looked at the dining room, the exercise room and the rec room."

"I want murals in my bedroom, a utility room and the kitchen dining area. That should cover it."

His bedroom. Her stomach grew fluttery at the thought. If only he would return to work in another city instead of staying at his Houston house, but she expected him to stick around to see what she was doing. She wished his bedroom wasn't one of the rooms.

"How soon can you start?" he asked. "I'd like to have them started right away."

"I have a job that's pending, but it's something someone in my office can handle," she said.

"Don't give my projects to someone else in your office. I'll have a contract drawn up and I want your efforts exclusively."

"I'm the only one doing the murals. That's something I've specialized in and I enjoy, so of course, I'll do the design and drawings myself. The work will go faster if someone helps me with the painting."

He shook his head. "No, unless it's errands and setting up equipment and that type of thing. Otherwise, I'm paying for you only," he said firmly.

"Fair enough," she replied.

A look passed between them that made her sizzle. Then he stepped closer to place his hands on her waist. "This is good. I've seen your work and you're talented. I admire the mural you did in San Francisco at the Haywind store and I saw a couple you did in Kansas City and one in San Antonio."

"I'm glad you liked what you saw," she said. She was aware of Cade's hands resting lightly on her waist as she looked up at him. They stood too close, conjuring up memories of other times she had stood with him like this.

"You can start right away?" he asked and his voice had dropped a notch, the only indication that he noticed anything else between them.

"Yes, I can," she said, stepping away from him. "Is your house far enough along for me to start drawing?"

"Yes," he replied, pulling on his coat. "We can talk about it while we eat dinner. Let's get back to the club," he said, and she crossed the room to pick up her purse, relieved that they were leaving his hotel suite and she would once again be out in public where the situation could not get intensely personal.

They had been seated only a short time back in the Millington Club when a first course of pan-seared crab cakes was served.

"We're so civilized," she said quietly while she ate a small bite. "I want to scream at you and throw things at you instead of work for you. As it is, you've bought yourself peace because I can't do that and work for you afterward."

He arched an eyebrow and his gaze drifted over her features. "For right now, perhaps we can both put the past on hold. It may not last, but we can try."

She inhaled, thought about the price he was willing to pay her and what she could do with the fortune. All her life she had been in competition with her brothers and even with her father. Now, her earnings would equal theirs. The mural earnings would give her a chance for spectacular accomplishments in her career.

If only she could hold to those thoughts and shove the past into oblivion, she might get through this assignment without unleashing all her pent-up fury that increased every time Cade indicated that there was reason for him to be angry with her over the past.

He couldn't have a single reason to have any bitterness on his part and it mystified her and infuriated her when he said that he did, but she didn't want to go into it because she'd already lost control once tonight, she didn't want to again.

"Tomorrow morning, if you're available, we can fly to Houston and return in the afternoon."

"That's fine," she replied as the waiter removed their dishes and brought green salads. Tomorrow she would spend the day with him. Her appetite had fled and she sipped her water.

"In your bedroom," she said, "the painting should be something pleasing and relaxing, something you really like. What do you enjoy?"

"I don't think you're going to want to paint that on my wall," he drawled, and she had to laugh in spite of her irritation. She didn't want his charm. Keep the barriers, she reminded herself.

"What are some of your favorite things?" she asked. "It used to be bikes, tinkering with cars and baseball, but, of course, I don't know what you like now."

"I haven't changed that much. My fascination with bikes has changed to cars. I enjoy baseball. Now I can enjoy things I couldn't then. I like fishing, skiing, golf, mountain climbing and snow boarding. As far as a subject for a mural for my bedroom—I'll have to think about that," he replied.

"I'll come up with possibilities for the subjects, too. That's my job."

As they talked about business and about the murals, she noticed he didn't have a big appetite, either. They kept the conversation off anything personal and she repeatedly thought about her job and changes she could make because of the money that would pour into her business, yet her train of thought wandered constantly back to Cade. Why hadn't he married? Why wasn't there a woman in his life now?

She shoved her questions aside. She wanted to keep everything as impersonal and professional as possible between them. He was now her client and she had to try to keep the past out of mind as long as she worked for him. Do the job and avoid thinking about their history—how many times would she have to remind herself? Had he ever loved her or had it all been a lie?

She took a deep breath and drank her water, trying to cool down and stop recalling the past, but she could only let go of memories a few minutes at a time and then soon, they were back in her thoughts again. She tried to pay attention to what he was saying as they talked in generalities and he inquired about different jobs she'd had, but her mind wandered. When her attention went to his mouth, she remembered his hot possessive kisses.

"You're not eating," he observed, drawing her abruptly back to the present. She felt her cheeks flush and hated that she couldn't control her blush.

"You haven't eaten very much yourself," she replied. "I'm tense anyway when I start a new job and maybe even more edgy tonight," she said.

"Relax," he said, reaching across the table to take her hand. "I'm no ogre to work for and I know you're an artist."

He held her hand, his thumb running back and forth lightly over her hand and then her wrist and she knew he probably felt her racing pulse. His dark eyes bore into her and their surroundings ceased to exist for her, leaving only Cade.

"Katherine," he said coaxingly, and for an instant, she wanted to lean closer to him until she realized how she was responding.

"Stop, it. I suppose it's from not seeing anyone for a long time, but I'm more susceptible than I want to be. You show some restraint or this isn't going to work."

"Sure, it'll work," he said softly.

They each left a large portion of their dinners untouched. The evening was a strain, and she was ready for it to end before she lost her composure with him again.

"Want to dance?" he asked, gazing at her with a level, flat stare that made her wonder what he felt and what was going through his mind.

"No, I don't, Cade. Let's keep anything between us strictly business."

"You know I paid royally for this evening with you," he said easily. "I haven't danced in a while. It seems to me, the night should include at least a dance," he said, standing and coming around the table. He pulled out her chair and she stood, trying to bite back her comments.

"You're definitely accustomed to getting your way," she said, standing, her pulse racing at the thought of dancing with him. Everything involving him was two-sided. Attraction caused her nerves to sizzle while anger kept her in a knot as she struggled to avoid another outburst with him.

He led her to the dance floor and the moment she walked into his embrace, her pulse jumped. Why did this seem so right? He held her close against him, and she felt the soft wool of his tux. She could detect the scent of his aftershave, feel the brush of his thighs against hers.

She danced with him as if time had vanished and it was nine years earlier. Every step was familiar, every move was seduction. Her heart pounded and heat burned inside her. They danced together in perfect coordination as if they had been dancing together every night for the whole nine years.

"This is good, Katherine, to hold you," he whispered, and his breath was warm against her ear. Her arm curled across his shoulder and she was careful to keep her hand on his coat and to avoid touching his neck. He swung her down in a dip and she instinctively clung to him as she looked into his dark eyes. She wanted him and there was no stopping what she felt.

In silence, she danced with him, closing her eyes only to be carried back in time again, remembering seductive moments in his arms when she had been wildly in love.

His arm tightened around her waist, pulling her closer. It was pure torment because they fit too well, moved together in perfect rhythm and every step stirred up damnable memories of dances in the past…seduction…Cade kissing her.

The instant the dance ended, she turned to walk back to the table. She tingled all over from being in his arms. Dancing together had stirred too many memories and sent desire to scalding levels.

Physically, she wanted to kiss and love him. She almost groaned out loud, caught herself and coughed, hoping she could cover the sound she had made.

She picked up her purse and faced him. "I know you paid a fortune for the evening, but as soon as possible, I'd like to end it. After all, you accomplished what you intended when I agreed to work for you."

"That's true," he said, taking her arm. "We'll go."

In the limousine he sat beside her again, closer this time, turning to face her. "I gave your address to the driver. I thought you'd live at the ranch."

"No, I moved out nine years ago and got an apartment. Now I own my own house and live in town. I have a house at the ranch. All of us do and Dad has given all of us land. We get together about twice a month, if possible."

"Nick told me he sees you fairly often."

Startled, she looked at Cade. "You sound as if you know Nick."

He shrugged. "Because of business dealings, we've crossed paths a few times."

She was startled to learn Nick had never mentioned Cade to her and wondered why he hadn't, deciding Nick probably thought it would be painful for her.

"I'm surprised he's civil to you," she said. "When you left, my brothers weren't living here at the time. If you remember, they were both in college. When they found out what you'd done, they went after you, but you and your family had left the state and they couldn't find you, which was a relief."

"That's not surprising."

Trying to avoid the past, she thought about her new job. "Actually I can be free right away to start thinking about your murals."

"Do you have someone you can really trust to run things if you're gone a long time?"

"Yes. I've been away for jobs a lot. Also, Houston to Fort Worth isn't so far that I can't get back if I have to."

"That's fine," he said easily, gazing intently at her. He wasn't touching her, but he still could set her aflame with his sexy brown eyes and his supercharged presence.

"Are you an early riser? I can pick you up and we'll go in my plane to Houston tomorrow. Is seven too early?"

"Seven works."

"Fine. That's a good time to go."

"Tomorrow I'll get your address and location," she said. "I'll find a motel nearby where I can set up my office and I can stay."

"No, that won't be necessary at all," he answered easily.

"Why not? I'm not commuting every day."

"Of course not. You don't need to commute. You'll live at my place," he replied.

Three

"No! I can't live with you," she snapped, twisting in the seat to face him, angry that he even suggested it.

"Of course you can stay at my place instead of a hotel," he replied smoothly. "You won't be 'living with me,' you'll be residing at my house," he said, unfastening his coat and pushing it open. "There's a world of rooms. Thirty rooms, as a matter of fact. You'll be right where you're working. If you don't want to bring your car, I can put one at your disposal. There's no reason not to stay there."

There were a dozen good reasons to avoid staying at his house, not the least of which was that the man was larger than life to her. Whether she liked it or not, she could never view him as she did other men. His touch was fiery and his look could hold her immobile. Her pulse was faster right now, just riding in the limo beside him. She was too susceptible to him, far too vulnerable.

Each minute with him compounded the attraction that tugged at her senses.

"Stop worrying, Katherine," he said quietly. "I'm no ogre. I'll be at work. The place is huge."

"I didn't expect to ever see you again. Now the idea of working for you, living under the same roof, spending time together, is unsettling. Give me as much space and solitude as possible. Your murals will turn out better, I'm sure."

"Is that a roundabout threat to leave you alone?"

"Not at all. I'm simply telling you that I'll work more efficiently under those conditions," she said, wanting to keep as much distance as possible between them.

He leaned close and drew his finger along her hand, making her tingle. "Let's not argue every step of the way. I'm paying you a fortune. In return, I want cooperation."

"Do you ever hear 'no'?"

"Occasionally, and if there's a logical reason, I pay attention. Can you give me a sensible cause for not staying at my place to do your painting?"

She gazed into his dark eyes. "You're giving me one good reason right now. You're too close. You're touching me constantly."

"Why is all that bad?" he asked.

"I'm susceptible to you, dammit, and I don't want to be. Does that make you feel better? Give me room."

He leaned away, his gaze intent. "I'll give you room, and you move into my house. It's large enough, Katherine. You'll see tomorrow."

Knowing she couldn't refuse to cooperate with him when he was being reasonable, she shrugged. "All right, Cade. I'll have to get measurements. I would prefer to look at all the rooms and then to focus on one at a time. I'll get a proposal put together for you and we can meet at my office to go over it."

"Sounds fine," he said. They turned into her gated area,

passed through the graceful white metal gates with Cade's driver using the combination she had given Cade on her card. They slowed and stopped in front of her one-story redbrick house that was set back in a landscaped yard with oak trees.

"Beautiful trees and house, Katherine," Cade said as he walked her to her door.

On the porch she faced him. "Thank you for your bid, for dinner and for your job offer. You've helped a lot of children tonight and you've given me a wonderful job opportunity."

"I'll get my money's worth," he said softly.

She frowned. "I hope there's no innuendo in your statement. You'll get six murals, nothing else. My body isn't included."

"I didn't expect it to be," he said, standing too close, gazing at her too intently.

For a few seconds they stared at each other. Her pulse raced and she could remember too many times he had kissed her good-night. Hastily, she removed her key and turned to open her door. Stepping inside, she switched off her alarm and turned back to find him standing in the open doorway. She had no intention of inviting him inside.

"Good night, Katherine. I'm looking forward to your work," he said, holding out his hand.

Reluctantly, she reached out to shake hands with him and had that electric sizzle that spun to her toes the instant his hand closed around hers. She wanted to yank her hand away, but instead, she merely withdrew it gently after a second. She didn't want this intense, fiery reaction to him, but there was no stopping it or keeping it from happening.

She watched him stride back to the waiting limousine. She closed the front door and leaned back against it, rubbing her forehead. Was he going to break her heart a second time?

She was going to live in his house and he would be there, watching what she was doing. All evening the question had plagued her of how she could resist him. Could she cope with being around him and not succumb to seduction?

Why was she so certain he would try to seduce her?

She could be wrong, but he hadn't done too well at keeping his hands off her tonight. She was equally uncertain whether she could continually hold her fury in check. He stirred opposing emotions in her constantly. One minute she was attracted, afraid she would fall in love again, the next minute she was fighting to control her temper.

She thought about when she had lost her temper with him tonight. At least the outburst had been brief. When she moved into his house, she hoped she could remain coolly professional with him and avoid him when she wasn't working.

She was drained and exhilarated all at once. Cade was here! She wished she could shake him right out of mind, but it was impossible. Everything inside her screamed a reminder that he had returned. After nine long years, Cade was back!

And then she thought about the murals and the payment she would get.

Her eyes flew open. Ten million dollars! She spun around in a circle, flinging out her arms and letting her purse fly, not caring when it hit the door and fell on the polished oak floor. She could open more offices—one at a time so she could get them started and running well before she moved on to another one. It had been her dream and now she would be able to do all she had planned.

Certain sleep was impossible, she kicked off her shoes and hurried to the office she had in her house. Switching on lights, she entered a room that was lined with shelves filled with books, drawings and awards. Two computers sat on her desk and another on a table.

She got down some books to look at pictures that might inspire her or trigger an idea.

As she poured over the pictures, her thoughts kept slipping

back to Cade and the time she had just spent with him, remembering dancing with him, being held in his arms again, something she had never expected to have happen.

Where had he made his fortune? Why was he angry with her? Why had he been so insistent that she take the job instead of another painter? She knew there were others who were as good as she was and he could have hired someone for far less. Why was he still single when he was so handsome and successful? Questions besieged her and she recalled that first moment she looked into his brown eyes and recognized him—everything inside her had clamored for her to throw herself in his arms. She was going to live in his house with him. The thought alone set her pulse racing. The house would be a palace, but if it were five times the size of a hotel, it wouldn't be large enough to keep fireworks from exploding between them.

Sooner or later, the past would rise up and all the money in the world couldn't keep it from happening. Shutting her eyes, she remembered how they had met. Clearly, she could recall hot, mid-afternoon July sunshine. She was home from college after her sophomore year, twenty years old. With the radio blaring, she was driving a battered pickup, the oldest on the Ransome ranch. Racing ten miles over the speed limit on the usually deserted county road, she sang as she headed home.

A truck passed driven by a cowboy, who honked and waved. It wasn't anyone she recognized, but she waved in return because most people who traveled the road lived somewhere in the general area.

Next she heard a bike and saw a guy on a Harley behind her. His shaggy, black hair was blowing behind him. He wore a red headband, a ragged T-shirt and frayed jeans. He pulled alongside her and honked.

She glanced at him, saw he was good-looking, so she smiled and then turned back to driving. He honked again and she flashed him a look.

Since she had been twelve years old, she had been receiving attention from males, so she was accustomed to honks, whistles, smiles, waves and guys hitting on her.

The biker wasn't anyone she knew. He persisted and then when he didn't get much reaction from her, he pulled ahead of her and slowed, causing her to slow or else she would hit him. When she signaled to pass him, he waved one arm frantically and as she tried to pass, he pulled over so she couldn't.

Annoyed, she started to pull to the right to try to pass him, but he swung over to the right and kept waving his arm, only now he was pointing and jabbing the air to his right with his index finger. If he wanted her to stop, he was crazy.

She wasn't afraid because she knew most people in her county and the surrounding area. She had her cell phone ready if she needed help.

He slowed, blocking her path.

She leaned on her horn and got within an inch of the back of his bike as they still drove down the highway, only now going below the speed limit. He shook his head, peeled out of her way and she pushed the accelerator, racing past him, sticking her tongue out at him as she roared past.

She glanced in her rearview mirror, saw him pull off to the side of the road and point to the right with a repeated jabbing sign. She was far enough past him, that if he was up to no good, she could get away, so she slowed, pulled off the deserted road to the shoulder. The pickup rolled to a stop and she climbed out, walking to the back. She glanced at the bed of the pickup and swore.

She heard the bike and turned to see him riding toward her. She knew now he'd been trying to help so her concern about him evaporated as she peered beyond him down the road.

He pulled up and stopped, cut his motor and swung his leg over his bike to climb off and walk up to her.

With midnight brown eyes, thick black hair, a firm jaw and

prominent cheekbones, he was the best-looking guy she'd ever seen and she couldn't keep from staring at him. She became conscious of her low-cut, faded and torn cutoffs, her T-shirt that ended inches above her small waist. His gaze raked over her in a blatant male assessment that made her tingle all over. Fire streaked in her and she became totally aware of him. Her gaze roamed down to his mouth, to his full sensual underlip. His shoulders were broad and he bulged with muscles and his powerful chest tapered down to a flat stomach, narrow hips and long legs.

She realized how she was looking him over and jerked her gaze up to see a heated look in his eyes and a faint, mocking smile lifting one corner of his mouth.

Her heart pounded as he strolled closer and stopped only inches in front of her. "I'm Cade Logan. You're—"

He waited, and she drew her breath. "Katherine Ransome," she said breathlessly, wondering what was happening. She never had such a volatile response to any guy. She felt weak-kneed, fluttery inside, and she tried to stop staring at him.

"Are you Matt Ransome's sister, Katherine?" he asked.

"Yes. You know Matt?"

He shrugged, a lazy lift of his shoulder that was as sensual as everything else about him. "We went to school together at Rincon High. I was a year ahead of Matt. I'm twenty-four now, and you're—?"

"Old enough to know what I like to do," she answered with a grin, suddenly wanting to flirt with him. His chest expanded as he drew a deep breath.

He gazed at her with hot speculation in his eyes. "I think I'm going to have to find out exactly what you like," he drawled in a husky voice that curled her toes. "But we'll have to postpone that discovery a bit. You've got bales—"

"The hay!" she exclaimed, remembering that her pickup now held only half the bales of hay it had held when she left town.

One dark eyebrow arched wickedly. "Made you forget your hay, didn't I," he drawled, and her gaze snapped back to him.

She slanted him a look, flirting with him again. "Might have, as a matter of fact. Hay isn't the most fascinating thing there is," she said in a languid drawl that caused a flicker in the depths of his eyes. "There are other things much more exciting to me."

"So what excites you, Katherine?" he asked, his innuendo unmistakable and her pulse drummed. As the question hovered between them, she looked at his mouth.

"Lots of things, but I don't do them with strangers. Or discuss them."

"So someone has to get to know you—I'll agree with that."

She smiled, and one corner of his mouth quirked in a crooked grin as he reached out to touch her cheek. "I didn't know why you were honking and waving," she said.

His mouth curled up in a knowing grin and he gave her another swift appraisal. "You're probably so used to guys honking at you that you barely notice."

She drew a deep breath, making her breasts strain against her T-shirt and seeing him lower his gaze. "You look like the type to honk and wave at a woman."

"Yeah," he said in a voice that had lowered a notch. "I like beautiful women, that's for sure. We can pursue this conversation later. Right now, you better get those bales off the road before someone has a wreck."

"Oh, my!" she said, realizing he was right and she'd forgotten the hay again. "Thanks," she called over her shoulder as she dashed toward the door of her pickup.

"I'll help you," he said and climbed on his bike.

She shrugged, climbed into the truck and made a U-turn to head back the way she came. She switched off the radio that had helped distract her from the falling bales of hay. Soon she spotted the first bale and a few others were scattered along the road just yards beyond.

She pulled off on the shoulder and he slowed to a stop behind her, coming around her truck. Before she could step out on the road, he took her arm to hold her back. "You drive on the shoulder and I'll pick 'em up and put them in your truck."

"This is the oldest, worst truck on the ranch and we don't usually drive it to town, but I was late and my car's in the shop, so I took it. I knew it was full of hay, but I didn't think the bales would bounce out."

"You should get the tailgate closed good."

"It's broken," she said. "Maybe now Dad will get rid of this clunker, but it's all right for ranch driving."

"This road's bumpy and filled with potholes so that added to your problem. Going over eighty didn't help, either. You're a fast woman, Katherine Ransome."

His sexy remark slithered across her nerves and made her tingle. She tilted up her chin.

"Only when I want to be," she answered, and he grinned.

"So what does it take to make you want to be? I may have to explore that one later. Right now, I'll get those bales."

Cade ran out into the road and picked up a bale to toss it into the back of her pickup. She climbed inside and drove slowly beside the road while he picked up more bales. His muscles flexed, pulling his T-shirt taut, and she drew a deep breath. He was strong, fit and appealing.

When there were no more bales in sight, he came around to her window.

"I think you have more back down the road. You've lost a bunch. Every time you'd hit a bump one would go out. I'll hide my bike off the road in the bushes and go with you to help you."

"Your bike will be stolen if you do."

"I'll take a chance," he said.

"Besides, I can lift a bale of hay when they're this size."

"I can lift them easier. You wait right here for me," he said and was gone to move his bike. She was tempted to drive off, but she was more tempted to wait and spend the time with him.

When he slid into the seat beside her, she drove back onto the road. Aware he sat and watched her, she tingled. "Sure of yourself, aren't you?"

He shrugged. "Sometimes."

"There are some more," she said, seeing bales ahead in the road. "I don't know how many were back there. Thank goodness there's so little traffic. We passed one car and he must have swerved around all of these."

"Where'd you drive from today?" Cade asked.

"Rincon," she replied.

"So did I. If you've just driven from Rincon, these are the first bales you lost because I didn't see any before this bridge."

She slowed, pulled onto the shoulder and climbed out. "I can help you," she said.

Before she picked up a bale, she yanked a bandana from her pocket. Catching her blond hair in her hand, she reached up to tie her hair behind her head with the bandana. As she did, he watched her intently, his gaze lowering to her breasts when her T-shirt pulled tautly against them.

She yanked the handkerchief into a knot. "There! I'm ready."

"So am I now," he said in a husky tone that gave a double entendre to his statement and she drew a deep breath. He was handsome and sexy, a lethal combination to a female heart. She wondered who he was and where he lived. Cade Logan meant nothing to her.

When the pickup was loaded, Cade climbed into the back and pushed the bales against the cab. "Now if you'll slow down, watch the bumps and potholes and keep your eye on these, you should get home with everything intact. I can follow you and see that you do," he said, jumping down beside her.

He dropped lightly to his feet like a cat and she was aware of how fit he was.

"Thanks for helping me," she said.

"Sure. Want to meet me for a burger tomorrow at lunch?" he asked, his brown eyes focusing intently on her.

She had a split second debate with herself because there was a raw sexuality to him that made her suspect if she had lunch with him, it would lead to more.

His eyes narrowed. "Are you scared to?"

She looked into his dancing dark eyes that were filled with speculation. "No, I'm not scared," she replied with a toss of her head. "I'll meet you at noon at Judd's."

"See you then, Katie," he said and drew his finger along her arm. He turned, climbed on his bike, revved the motor and was gone.

Remembering, she was astounded again how far he had come from where he had been back then. When she had met him, he lived with his family of four boys and no father in a dilapidated two-bedroom house that was in the poorest part of Rincon.

He was four years older than she was, and in high school she hadn't known him. Earning his living as a mechanic and buying and selling old cars on the side, he had dropped out of school his senior year, but he had known both of her brothers. From the day she had met Cade, she'd always thought he was the most exciting person she had ever met.

She vowed with every ounce of willpower she had that she would not fall in love with him a second time around and open herself to hurt like she had years ago.

Staring into space, she replayed over and over the past hours' events. She wanted to call her brothers to tell them the latest developments, but she would do that tomorrow before she left for Houston. Both of them were early risers and she could call after six.

She worked far into the night before she went to bed and fell asleep only to dream about Cade, dreams of kisses and lovemaking that left her in a bigger turmoil when she awoke the next morning.

She showered and dressed, wearing a navy suit and pumps because she was determined to look professional to try to keep a wall between them. With care she looped and pinned her blond hair on her head.

About fifteen minutes before Cade was to pick her up, she called her brother and after two rings heard his deep voice. "Nick. It's Katherine. I'm leaving town and wanted to talk to you first."

"How'd the auction go?"

"It was very good. They made a lot of money."

"Great! Glad to hear it and Julia will be, too. Who bid for you?" he asked with amusement in his voice. "I'll bet Hank Monroe did. I wonder if he'll still be trying to go out with you when you're sixty years old," Nick remarked and laughed at his own statement.

"Several men bid," she replied casually. "Cade Logan is back. He won the bid and the evening with me. We went to dinner last night."

She held the phone away from her ear while her brother swore. "Why'd you go out with Cade Logan?"

"Because he was the highest bidder, Nick," she said patiently.

"You sound damned happy about it," Nick snapped. "It's not back on between the two of you, is it?"

"No! I'm going to work for Cade. He made me the prover- bial offer I couldn't refuse," she said, her pulse jumping at the thought of announcing her client's offer to her brothers.

"It must have been damn high," Nick said, sounding grumpy over the phone. "I'd like to beat him to a pulp, Katherine."

"Well, don't. You'd go to jail, and I'd lose a lucrative contract that will set me up in my business in a way I never dreamed possible."

"Okay, how much?" Nick asked, and she wished she could see his face.

"Cade has a new home in Houston and he wants me to paint six murals in it."

"And— C'mon. He must be paying you a fortune for you to take the job and sound cheerful today."

"How's ten million for the six murals?"

She held the phone away from her ear again as Nick swore and whistled loudly and yelled to Julia to come let Katherine tell her something. Next, she had to tell her sister-in-law, Julia, about the deal she had made with Cade. Then Nick was back on the phone.

"You've made a bargain with the devil," Nick snapped. "But for that sum, I don't blame you. I knew he was doing well, but I didn't know it was that good. How in sweet hell has he made that kind of money?"

"Look who's asking," she said, momentarily amused because Nick had made a huge fortune in only a few years.

"I had backing to start. I had Dad and his finances and a bit on my own and an education, et cetera, et cetera. Cade had nothing. Worse than nothing. He had a bad background."

"Don't build him up," she said dryly.

"Dammit, he's going to break your heart again. Is he married?"

"No, he won't break my heart and no, he's not married. This is the deal of a lifetime. I'll be careful."

"Yeah, right. And we'll try to pick up the pieces later."

"Ridiculous! I'm over him," she announced, but her words were hollow and conjured up her racing pulse and pounding heart and breathlessness too many times the night before. "This morning he's flying me to Houston to see his house. You can get me on my cell phone if you need to."

"For ten million, he wants you a hell of a lot. I know you're good at what you do, but Katherine, he's coming after you."

"No, he's not. He just thinks I'm good at murals."

"I know you're damned good, but you don't command prices like that."

"I might now," she said with glee, always feeling a competitive edge with her brothers even though she loved them dearly.

"I hope the job is worth what you get."

"It's going to be, Nick. I have plans."

"You be careful and if you want me, call anytime."

"You sound as if I'm walking into danger."

"I just remember what you went through before."

She glanced at her watch. "Gotta run. Thanks, Nick, for being the brother you are. I'd like to tell Matt and Dad about my deal."

"I don't blame you except give me time to drive out to Dad's place. I'll leave in thirty minutes. He'll be in such shock that he might have a heart attack."

"No, he won't. You don't have to go there. I'll break the news easily," she said, smiling. "Better run." She closed off the conversation and called Matt to tell him and listened to his ire change to shock over the fee she would receive. She let Matt talk her into allowing both brothers to break the news to their dad. She knew her father despised Cade and she decided Matt probably knew best, so she told him to go ahead and she would call their father later.

Chimes rang and she hurried to the door. In a short-sleeved black knit shirt and charcoal slacks, Cade was as handsome as ever, only now, the knit shirt revealed powerful shoulders and bulging biceps that ignited a flame.

Heightening her reaction, his gaze drifted slowly and appreciatively over her.

"Good morning," he said and his voice was husky, causing an unwanted sizzle. "Sleep all right?" he asked.

"I slept great," she replied emphatically with a twinge of conscience over the uncustomary lie, but she had no intention of informing him that he had destroyed her sleep and her peace.

"You look beautiful this morning, but you could have dressed casually, and you could have left your hair down," he added, touching locks of her hair.

"Thank you. You're a client now, and this is a business trip, so I selected clothes accordingly," she replied. "I have to close the door to activate my alarm and then I'm ready to go," she said.

He draped one hand over her head on the doorjamb and leaned closer, and her pulse had another rush. "I'm causing you to activate your alarm?" he drawled in a voice that made her forget her house alarm totally.

"Don't flirt, Cade," she said breathlessly, wanting to flirt back with him, annoyed that he would tease her. "We're not going there again."

"With you it's difficult to avoid," he said, his voice changing as he dropped his arm and turned his back.

She glared at his back, realizing he had the same mixture of anger and attraction that she experienced.

When the alarm was set, she emerged, and closed and locked the door. He took her arm to walk to the limo. Another touch on her arm—the constant physical contacts with him had commenced again and fueled fires that had started yesterday in her. As she sat down and crossed her legs, she looked up to catch him watching her.

"So why are you building a house in Houston?" she asked him while they drove away from her house.

"I bought an oil company that has its headquarters there. Houston has a lot of possibilities for me."

"From what I've read about you, you buy and sell companies. Do you always move where you invest?"

"No, I don't." He rubbed the back of his neck as if he were battling some inner turmoil, and she let it drop and rode in silence. "This is my home state, and I wanted to come back and see what things are like after nine years," he explained.

"I'll have to admit that I couldn't resist letting hometown folks see that I've done all right."

"With the astronomical donation you made last night to the children's charity, I'm sure you'll impress all the hometown folks. The auction is written up in the morning paper and you've shown everybody how successful you've been."

"That wasn't the point of my high bid," he said dryly. "It was to get you out with me again so I could make my offer."

"You succeeded in not only getting me out with you, but in talking me into taking you as a client."

"Not many people would have turned down my offer," he remarked. "If the auction is in the paper, someone may get curious about my bid for you and our past history and we may become interesting to the media."

"I hope not," she said with a shudder. "I don't want the past dredged up again. The bachelorette auction had a small article in the society section this morning, because they cover fancy charity events. There are a few pictures, but not ours, thank heaven!"

"That may not be the end of news about us if any reporter with a memory gets hold of the story."

She tilted her head and stared at him. "So you came back to show everyone how well you've done."

"I came because of business. I'll admit, I hope some of the people I grew up with in Rincon know about my new house. Foolish as it is, there's a part of me that has to prove something. I had some rough times," he replied.

"I know you did," Katherine said quietly as she tried to ignore memories of his struggles and his family's poverty while hers had wealth. She didn't want him to stir her sympathy, but she knew too well that he'd had tough years when he was growing up.

"So you built in Houston to impress the home folks," she repeated.

"I guess it's ego, Katherine. Otherwise, I probably would have just purchased a condo. A condo would have been sufficient for business. If you recall, everybody thought I'd turn out badly."

"I never did think you would," she declared, and he looked into her eyes in a fiery gaze that startled her with its smoldering anger.

"You said you didn't," he stated with so much cynicism, her surprise grew.

"And you think in truth, that I did?" she asked. "Do you think I intended to marry someone I thought was bad? Why on earth would I do that?"

"Rebellion," he replied quietly.

"That's absurd, Cade. Rebelling against what?" she asked, astounded by his reply.

"Your father. I remember how you fought him."

"If I'd married you to get back at him, it would just spite myself."

"You wouldn't be the first. You told me how all of you clashed constantly with him. You said Nick and Matt fought him when they were growing up and that's why Nick left as soon as he could."

"I argued with my dad over dating you," she said, gazing into Cade's angry dark eyes. "But I didn't go out with you because of anger at my dad. Not ever."

"Do you remember what you felt when you were twenty?" Cade asked, and his voice dripped with sarcasm.

"I remember precisely," she snapped.

The limo stopped, interrupting their conversation that had done nothing to mollify her anger with him. She dismissed Cade's answer to her about rebellion because that had never been a reason for her to see him.

At the Fort Worth business airport Cade exited the limo and turned to help her. Yards away, a sleek, white Learjet waited.

Ignoring Cade's outstretched hand, Katherine emerged into warm sunshine. She wanted to do everything for herself, to stop the physical contacts that were pure fire. She hated that she still found him appealing and despised the instant bone-deep response to him when they touched each other. Every look, each touch was electrifying and unwanted to her and now she was going to his house to live. A big mural could take almost two weeks. She was facing possibly more than two months with him. She inhaled, lecturing herself on resistance.

To avoid his taking her arm, she strode ahead of him and climbed the stairs into the jet. The moment he stepped inside the luxurious plane, Cade dropped his hand on her shoulder.

"Sit where you want. I'll speak to our pilot and then join you."

Drawing a deep breath, she watched him go through the plane. There was no stopping her racing pulse. Was getting involved with Cade again going to be worth all the money she was making?

With another deep breath she pulled her gaze from his purposeful stride and selected a cushioned chair that gave her a window view. In minutes he returned to sit facing her, stretching his long legs out in front of him, almost touching hers.

"This will be a little over an hour and a half flight, so you can relax."

She wondered if she could ever relax around him, but she wouldn't tell him. His cell phone rang and she turned to look out the window again while snatches of his conversation indicated he had a business call.

Glancing at Cade while he talked, she was surprised to find him watching her. She turned back to the window.

She wanted to demand that he tell her why he had walked out on her, but at the same time, she wanted him to explain without her having to ask. Why had she foolishly expected an explanation and an apology? She had thought she was over him and had forgotten him, until last night when she looked up into his eyes and time fell away and she knew then, in some ways the years didn't matter. The hurt and the attraction remained. Forgetting and indifference were impossible. Something had stirred his anger at her, as well, and she couldn't imagine what.

The pilot announced they had been cleared for takeoff. Katherine and Cade were buckled in and she looked out the window as they gained speed, then they were airborne.

Chatting politely with Cade, she couldn't concentrate on what was being said. Her thoughts jumped to business possibilities while her physical awareness of Cade ignited memories. As their small talk barely registered, she watched Cade, his long legs and well-shaped hands. Trying to focus on the task ahead, she attempted to sound him out on what kind of art work he preferred, realizing he had eclectic tastes.

"You've done amazingly well in nine years," she observed, wondering about him. "You left here with nothing."

His dark eyes flashed in an expression that puzzled her, and she suspected she had said something that angered him, but she didn't know why.

"How did you get where you are today?" she asked.

Four

"When I left here we went to California. About as far as we could get in this country."

"Who's 'we'?" she asked even though she was certain of his answer, but now that they were into the past, she couldn't keep from inquiring. "Your whole family?"

"Yes. We all left here together," he replied and her curiosity increased. For nine years she had speculated why he might have walked out like he did, but she could never come up with a reason for him to have left without telling her.

"We drifted across the country and went to L.A. For a few months I held odd jobs, but then I was fortunate to land employment with Edwin Talcott, a multimillionaire entrepreneur and financier. I became his chauffeur, as well as sort of a handyman and mechanic for his cars. Occasionally, I helped his gardener."

"You've come a long way from chauffeur and gardener," Katherine remarked, wondering what had happened in the intervening years. She glanced again at his hands, that weren't the hands of a gardener.

"Edwin decided I had some sense and he started helping me, teaching me things and sending me to college. I was a walk-on that first year and then I got a scholarship to play football and when it wasn't football season, I worked for him doing office work. I picked up what he was teaching me and with his help, I made some investments. When those grew, I made more. I didn't finish college because I was doing well with the investments and I worked for him."

"That's a leap to the point where you are today," she said, suspecting he was leaving events out of his story.

"Not really," Cade answered easily. "I went on my own and did even better. I've been lucky. Edwin didn't have any family and he left his fortune to me. I inherited it three years ago and since that time I've doubled the amount. Money generates money."

"Then it was better for you to leave here, wasn't it?" She gazed into his unfathomable brown eyes, and she couldn't guess what he was thinking, but she was surprised when she didn't receive an affirmative answer from him immediately.

"I suppose it depends on where you place your values," he replied finally, and her pulse jumped. Had he meant that he would have been better off staying here? She wondered. Did Cade have regrets? She shrugged away the notion because he could have come back in the intervening years.

"So where do you place your values?" she asked, surprised by his answer.

"Family is more important than income," he said and she stared in disbelief.

"All that you did since you left here has made you enormously wealthy while you're still young, plus given you some education," she said, not mentioning that the rough edges about him had disappeared. "If you'd stayed, you would have married. That you can do anyway, and I'm surprised you haven't already. Why haven't you married?" she asked. "Or is that getting too personal?"

"I never found anyone that I wanted to marry," he replied in a husky voice and gave her a piercing look that sizzled along her nerves and made her feel that in some manner, his statement was aimed directly her. "Why haven't you married?" he asked.

"I'm wed to my work," she replied. "That's where my time and attention goes."

To her surprise, he leaned forward to draw his fingers down her cheek and then he slipped his hand across her nape, sliding his fingers around to rest his hand on her throat. "Work doesn't take all your attention. Right now, your pulse is racing, Katherine. You're passionate and responsive. You're a gorgeous woman, and I know men have been in your life. There's a lot more to life than your work."

"And you're offering to reenter my life and show me what I've been missing? No, thank you," she replied, trying to hang on to her poise and hating that he could feel her racing pulse.

"No, I've no intention of getting us back together. We've got too many hurtful moments between us. I'm just surprised you're not married and curious why you're not," he said.

He was too close to her, and his dark gaze bore into her. She was aware of his fingers lightly pressing against her throat. She couldn't keep from looking at his mouth and then she jerked her gaze back to meet his. "If you're pushing for me to say I've been waiting for you to come back, give it up."

"Of course not. I'm amazed to find you single and no particular man in your life. You're too beautiful to sit home alone nights."

"Thank you for the compliment, but when I do get a chance to sit home alone, it's a relief to not have to do anything. There's no one, Cade, and I'm fine with that. You said there's no one in your life, either, so why tell me I need someone?" While she talked, his gaze drifted slowly over her features, making her tingle. He ran his index finger lightly across her lower lip.

"Don't get personal, Cade," she remarked and he leaned away, smiling at her.

"I didn't intend to disturb you."

"You don't disturb me!" she snapped. His eyebrow arched wickedly, and he gave her an amused look.

"I don't?" he asked, leaning close again to trail his hand along her arm. "That doesn't cause a jump in your pulse? I'll admit it," he said, with his voice becoming husky, "it makes mine race." He placed his hand on her throat. "Let me see if you're wrong, and I do disturb you—"

"All right, you know damned well you do!" she said, scooting back and getting a mocking grin from him. "Don't make much of it. I'm a woman and you're an attractive male."

"And you're getting angry over it. Enjoy the attraction."

"No, thanks. I don't want a relationship. I don't want a friendship. Either would be absolutely impossible."

He gazed at her solemnly and nodded. "You're beautiful and I—" He broke off abruptly. "There are moments when I forget all our past, but you're right." He clamped his jaw closed and turned away and she wondered what he had been about to say.

At Houston Hobby Airport they came down through clouds and rolled to a smooth stop. When the door opened, Cade took her arm lightly as wind buffeted them and thunder rumbled in the distance.

Instead of another waiting limousine, a chauffeur stepped out of a black sedan and handed the keys to Cade, who led her around to the passenger side to open the door for her.

As soon as she was seated, Cade circled the car and slid behind the wheel to drive. She buckled her seat belt and shifted slightly to watch him. He threaded through traffic winding through town and then into a residential area of increasingly larger homes.

She rode in silence, prickly, too aware of him, tingling from his touch. While she thought about what he'd just told her, she watched him drive.

Finally, they went through tall, black iron gates that had an attendant who waved at Cade. They followed a winding, tree-lined street with an occasional mansion set back on well-tended lawns. More gates swung open to Cade's private drive and as he wound along it, they passed an immaculate, emerald lawn shaded by tall oaks draped with feathery Spanish moss and magnolia trees. When they rounded a curve, a mansion spread before her in a setting of tall pines.

Stunned, she stared at a structure that awed her with its beauty and size that had been inadequately represented in the simple line drawings of his blueprints. Once again, he surprised her.

"It's a palace!" she exclaimed, looking at a three-story stone structure with slate roofs, mullion windows and huge wings spreading away to the east and west. Trucks of various types and sizes were parked near the west wing, and scaffolding and ladders were against the walls as workmen scrambled over the incomplete wing.

After the first shock at the size of the place and the elegant fountain in front and formal gardens, her second thought was that she and Cade would never see each other because the place was so huge, causing relief to swamp over her.

"How can you stay here all by yourself?" Instantly, she realized she shouldn't have inquired. "Sorry. I was out of place to ask you. It's none of my business. And you haven't lived here long, have you?"

"I don't mind your questions. No, I haven't stayed in the house a lot. The builders have finished, all except one wing and the guest house, and the decorator has finished part of the house so I have furniture, and the place is livable. As far as residing alone, I'm comfortable with a big place. Remember, I grew up with three brothers and two bedrooms."

"I know," she remarked, not adding that she recalled everything about him.

"All my houses are large and I guess it's because of my past. Plus, it's an investment. Perhaps the big houses are part security blanket, part a balm for my ego. You're the only person I've ever admitted that to," he said. "I'm not looking for sympathy because you know my past, but I don't ever want to be hungry or crowded again."

She inhaled, hating that she had gotten them on a personal basis because it did prompt her sympathy, which she didn't want to feel.

"Since it's your first visit, I'll take you in the front door," he said when he stopped the car.

"Trying to impress me?" she asked.

"Of course," he replied with a grin, and she couldn't resist smiling in return, while he climbed out and went around the car in long strides.

"Keep the conversation impersonal," she whispered to herself as she watched him. "Don't tell only me your inner feelings and motives," she added, knowing he couldn't hear her. When he opened her door, she stepped out of the car.

The mammoth porch and stately Corinthian columns were magnificent. He was building a showplace. Taking a deep breath, she walked along beside him as they crossed the porch and he touched a button beside a plate with an intercom.

"You don't carry a key?" she asked.

"Not to the front of any of my houses. If I carried all my keys, I'd jingle like a sleigh."

When the door swung open, a uniformed maid greeted Cade with a big smile.

"Good morning, Mr. Logan."

"Morning. Mrs. Wilkson, this is Miss Ransome, who'll be moving in soon to paint murals for me." He turned to Katherine. "This is Mrs. Wilkson, Katherine."

"I'm glad to meet you," Katherine said, stepping into the enormous, elegant entrance hall with marble floors and a soaring vaulted ceiling.

"Pleased to meet you, too, ma'am," Mrs. Wilson said as she closed the front door. Katherine was relieved to discover there would be other people in the mansion, but she should have guessed in such a large place, Cade would have help. She received more surprises when Cade took her arm and they walked along the hall.

"I'll introduce you to my staff," Cade said. "If you ever need to find one of them, their schedules are posted in the pantry," he added. While she wondered how big a staff he had, she was even more relieved that there would be several people present in the house and she wouldn't be alone with him.

"Where do they stay?" she asked, guessing they had quarters in the huge mansion, probably on the third floor.

"They have their own small houses," he answered, and she glanced up at him.

"I'm surprised. This place is huge. You could have had them stay here and they'd never be in your way. When I was growing up we had a live-in nanny and a live-in cook and a live-in maid. Their quarters were all on the top floor. Of course, the ranch was too far away for anyone to drive back and forth daily."

"I could've done that, too, but that isn't what I want," he answered evenly. "I intend for people who work for me to have their own places and their privacy. I want my staff to like their work. I treat them as I would want to be treated if I had their jobs."

She nodded. "That's because of your past," she observed.

"Damn straight, it is. I've been poor and done menial work

and know what it is to be treated like you're insignificant. I'm not knowingly doing that to anybody."

"So you don't adhere to the old adage, 'Familiarity breeds contempt.'"

"Not that kind of familiarity. I believe respect creates a better relationship."

"I can't argue that one," she said, remembering the small rooms that their help had when she was young.

Mouthwatering smells of baking bread and barbeque floated in the air, reminding her that she had eaten only a few bites of her breakfast.

They stepped into a state-of-the art kitchen with polished oak cabinets and granite countertops. Large windows let sunlight spill into the spacious room that opened into a living area with a stone fireplace, a sofa, chairs and a long, polished wooden table that would seat ten people. Near an oven, a short, barrel-chested man with a shiny bald head and toothy smile faced her.

"Katherine, this is Creighton, who's been with me several years and is one of the best chefs in the world. Creighton, meet Miss Ransome."

They talked politely for a moment and then Cade took her arm to steer her into the hall again. "Let's find your room and then you can have a tour of the finished part of my house."

"How many work for you here?"

He shrugged. "My gardener and his crew. One of them is a chauffeur when I need one. I have two cleaning people—one is Mrs. Wilkson. I have Creighton and I have a handyman."

She was astounded, but more reassured than ever that she wouldn't be alone with Cade often.

Her good feelings about avoiding him vanished when he showed her a suite that was to the left of the sweeping main staircase to the second floor.

As she entered the sitting room, he said, "This is where I

thought you might like to stay. The rooms across the hall can be used for your office and studio."

"Fine," she said, barely seeing the room because Cade stood close by her side. "And you stay where?" she asked, expecting him to be in the opposite end of their wing.

"My suite is next to this one."

She turned to stare at him. "In this enormous mansion, you're putting me next to you?"

"Don't worry, Katherine. I'll leave you alone," Cade answered, and this time the steel was clearly present and fire flashed in his dark eyes. "The west wing is under construction, so I can't stay in it. In this wing, these are the only two bedroom suites. If you don't want to stay in here, there are other smaller bedrooms down the hall."

"This is fine," she said, knowing there would be no avoiding him some of the time. "So we'll see each other and we'll be together," she said.

"Is contact between us a problem?" he asked, placing his hands on his hips and studying her. He moved closer and her pulse jumped. "Why is it a problem?"

"Cade, you've hired me to do a job for you, and I intend to do it. In the meantime, I'm trying to keep the lid on my anger with you. I'm not certain I'll be able to if we are constantly together."

"That was nine years ago," he reminded her, increasing her fury.

"You expect me to *forget?*" She flung the words at him, hurt boiling in her. "You simply left without a word—" She clamped her mouth closed, not wanting to go into the past, knowing if she started flinging accusations, she would say things she'd regret. She thought about the job he had hired her to do and knew she had to focus on it totally and forget everything else.

"Dammit, Katherine! You sound as if you think you were the only one hurt!" he snapped and a muscle worked in his jaw.

"You did just what you wanted to do, and you didn't tell me. There's nothing that would justify the way you walked out!" she cried, clenching her fists and shaking. "You hurt me in the worst possible way!"

"And were you in love with me, or just using me to get back at your father?"

"In the plane today I told you that was never any part of why I became engaged and intended to marry you. And I never expected you to turn out badly. I never saw you as bad."

"Oh, come on! At first you didn't let any of your family know you were seeing me. You sure as hell didn't let your brothers know."

"All right, I'll admit I didn't at first because you were wild and you had dropped out of school, which they wouldn't have liked. But it wasn't a big thing."

"The hell it wasn't."

She drew a deep breath. "I knew you were wild, but that's all. And I never once went out with you to get back at my dad. You're giving me a doubting look," she added with her anger increasing.

He shrugged one shoulder. "Maybe we should have had this conversation nine years ago, but my temper ruled my judgment and your father made a good case. I was—"

"My father!" she exclaimed. "What did my father have to do with making a 'good case' to you?"

"Plenty," he replied. "I was a boy then, defensive about my life. Your father told me that your interest in me was out of rebellion—that there wasn't any love," Cade snapped.

"You never told me that he talked to you," she said, astounded.

"Oh, he talked all right," Cade said, fury burning in his dark eyes.

"And without asking me, you believed him?"

"Damn straight I did. Why wouldn't I? I heard it from others. He said your brothers would say the same thing if I asked them. They weren't in town to ask. I didn't know them well and they were both away. But I knew how you fought with your father."

"You knew my father would do all sorts of things to get what he wanted—"

"And so would his daughter—"

Rage exploded in her and she reached out again to slap him. Just as deftly as before, Cade caught her wrist and yanked her up against him, holding her arm behind him. She was pressed tightly against his hard length, both of them breathing hard. "You always did have a temper, Katherine."

"Let go of me."

"Tell me you didn't want to marry me to get back at your father. You fought with him over everything that year."

"No! Damn you for believing him, and him for telling you such a thing!" With her free hand she pushed against Cade's shoulder, and it was like shoving a rock. Only she wasn't pressing against a rock, but warm, solid muscles. He shifted, releasing her wrist and wrapping her in his arms to hold her so tightly she could barely breathe.

"I was in love with you!" she cried.

"Then, dammit, after I left here, why didn't you take my calls or answer my letters?" he snapped.

"Why would I since you walked out without a word? I never wanted to see you again!" She looked up into his dark eyes that flashed with fire. She was held tightly against him while his scalding gaze devoured her. Anger burned away, and the moment transformed.

"No!" she whispered, but her protest was breathless, almost inaudible as she strained with her arms to get free of his grasp.

"Stand still, Katherine," he commanded as he looked intently at her.

His gaze lowered to her mouth and her heart slammed

against her ribs. "I remember absolutely what it was like to kiss you," he said.

Her heart thudded and heat flooded her, demolishing her anger because she, too, could remember exactly how it had been to kiss him. She looked at his mouth and then into his dark gaze and she was lost.

He leaned down, placing his mouth on hers and she went up in flames. Years and anger didn't exist. His kiss was seduction, sending jolts of electricity that fanned the flames already low inside her.

His hand went into her hair, and he released his other arm that circled her waist. When he did, she slipped her arms around his neck. Yielding to desire, she wanted to devour him and she felt as if that was what he was doing to her. He leaned over her, molding her against him while his kiss deepened and possessed, his tongue stroking her with fervor.

Craving pounded in her and she thrust her hips against him. She wanted him with a pent-up desperation of nine long years, a yearning that dimly shocked her, but had instantly spun out of control the moment his lips touched hers.

His kiss inflamed her. While her pulse roared, lights exploded behind her closed eyes. Aching for all of him, tremors shook her. Her world rocked and spun topsy-turvy. Wisdom was ashes and need was overwhelming.

Her hair tumbled down, but she was only dimly aware of it falling. His hand slid slowly down her back, a stroke that she could barely detect through her suit coat, but then she felt his hand roam over her bottom. He shifted her slightly, his hand drifting to her front, easing up over her hip and ribs.

Through her navy silk blouse, his fingers caressed her breast and rubbed her nipple, heightening her ecstasy and torment.

Powerful, relentless and seductive, his kiss awakened desires in her that she had thought were gone forever.

She knew that she had to slow him or they would be at the

point of no return and she would be mired in a legion of complications with him. Reason was vague, a faint nagging that she wanted to ignore. She ran her hands across Cade's broad shoulders and a sob tore from her throat, but was taken in his kiss—a kiss that she had dreamed about, longed for, tried to forget for so many years. His kiss burned her like a brand now and caused her hips to shift. She wanted him more than ever before.

His hands were beneath her blouse, cupping her breasts and then pushing away her bra, his fingers circling her nipples with fiery caresses that finally broke through the blanket of longing that enveloped her.

Moaning, she clutched his wrists, leaning back to look up at him. "You have to stop now!" she gasped.

Desire blazed in his dark eyes and took her breath. There was no question that he wanted her.

Was this what he had intended from the start—seduction? Was he coming back into her life only to break her heart all over again?

Was she going to let him?

She gasped for breath and noticed his breathing was as ragged as hers. His lips were red from their kiss, and his hungry gaze looked as if he wanted to consume her totally. He played with a lock of her hair.

"You burn me to cinders," he whispered, and her heart pounded. "That was the kiss of a lifetime," he added, shaking her even more. While she agreed with him, she wouldn't admit it. Aching to pull his head down and continue kissing, she clenched her fists. At the same time, her fury simmered, and now it was fueled by anger at herself for succumbing to him.

"We're not going there, Cade. Never again!"

"Shhh!" He placed his finger on her lips, and her heartbeat quickened.

"No, we're not," she said, snapping at him and jerking her head away. "If that's what you expected—"

"Just don't say 'never' about something as exciting as when we kiss." While he studied her features, he combed his fingers through her hair. "Your hair is soft," he whispered as the last pins fell around her feet.

She caught his wrist in her hand. "You know I can't turn down a fee worth millions, but I don't want this. I don't want your kisses—"

"You didn't act that way a minute ago," he drawled, one dark eyebrow arching.

"So I respond to you physically!" she snapped. "It's lust. I don't go out often with men. I'm vulnerable about some things, but I don't want to kiss," she said, tucking her silk blouse back into her skirt. "Look at me! I look—"

"Like you've been kissed," he said in a velvet tone that heated her. "You're more beautiful now than you used to be," he said.

"Thank you," she replied in clipped words, trying to ignore her racing pulse or the rush of pleasure over his compliment. "I don't want intimacy or to get close or to trust you that way again. You killed my trust and if you thought I didn't love you, you were wrong. If you thought my only reason for marrying you was because I was rebelling against my father and trying to get back at him, you should have told me. Leave me alone." She started to walk away, but he jerked her around to face him, holding her squarely by the shoulders.

"Dammit, Katherine, you don't even know what lengths your father went to, or why I left, and you never did care or even want to find out when I wrote and called."

"You keep talking about my father—so he talked to you and you believed him without even asking my side."

"He did a hell of a lot more than talk."

Surprised, she wondered if she were hearing the truth. In the past Cade had always been honest with her and there was no reason to deceive her now. He had already gotten what he really wanted from her—the agreement to paint his murals.

"What else? What else could my dad have done to make you walk out on our wedding?"

Five

"If he'd threatened you physically or beaten you up, that would have just made you all the more determined," she persisted.

"You're right and I'm sure he knew that."

"Then what was it?" she asked, unable to imagine her father doing anything to sway Cade, who had a stubborn streak.

"Time and again he offered to pay me off to get me to walk out."

"I don't believe you," she said, stunned at first, stepping back and staring at Cade who placed his hands on his hips. "My dad will go to great lengths to get what he wants, but he's never hurt any of us deeply in order to get his way. He wouldn't hurt me that way."

"Well, he did hurt you—or contribute to me hurting you. The first few times he offered to pay me off if I'd get out of your life, I turned him down."

"Why didn't you tell me?"

"I didn't see any reason to cause you more anger toward your dad."

"I don't believe you." She started to walk past Cade to leave the room and get away from him.

"The first time he offered me two hundred and fifty thousand dollars to leave the state."

She stopped with her back to him, wanting to throw her hands over her ears and rush out of the room to avoid hearing what she thought were lies, but she couldn't move.

"Then he offered four hundred thousand. He wanted me out of your life badly. One of the conditions, of course, was that you would never know. I'm breaking that condition right now."

She spun around. "You took the money?" she asked, barely able to get out the words because it meant Cade was telling the truth. She was stunned to know her father would hurt her like that. "I can't believe that the payment was worth more than our love. That's the deepest hurt of all, Cade. And I don't believe that my dad would hurt me so badly," she said without being aware she was saying the words aloud.

"He probably thought he was doing what was best for you and your future happiness. He damn well told me enough times that I was bad for you, I had nothing to offer you, no hope for the future. I would drag you down."

"You knew I didn't feel that way."

"Your father pointed out I had a brother in trouble with the law, no father in our family, no means to do anything for you, no future hope. I'd been in trouble at school for cutting classes. I was wild, poorly educated—he made it very clear that if I loved you, I'd get the hell out of your life."

Stunned, she chilled as she stared at Cade and knew he was telling her the truth. "I loved you and I wanted to marry you."

"You know your dad was partially right and at the time, I thought he was dead right about all of it. I didn't expect to go into the world and make a fortune—there's nothing in my background or anyone else in my family that indicated such a thing."

"You should have told me."

"You would have argued with me and said his accusations didn't matter—if you loved me. If you were rebelling as he said you were, you would have quarreled with me and said it didn't matter, too. Either way, your reaction would have been the same. At the time I did love you, Katherine, and I hurt because I thought you were marrying out of rebellion. It was easy to believe your dad. Except for actually telling me you wanted to marry me for that reason, you gave every indication of rebellion. You argued with your dad. We went out without you telling him who you were with. You complained to me how dictatorial he was. You did things he told you not to—taking the car when you weren't supposed to, calling me long distance when you weren't supposed to. You wore clothes that you knew he wouldn't approve of—do I need to continue? You know you were rebellious."

"So that's why you walked," she said, staring at him and wondering what would have happened if they had confronted each other with their accusations at the time. "You took four hundred thousand dollars in exchange to walk out on me." She knew Cade would have believed it when her dad told him he was nothing and would hurt her future because Cade had worried about that himself. And with the poverty of Cade's family, she could see where the money looked like a lifetime fortune to him, but she wouldn't have taken any amount to walk out on him. "I wouldn't have walked on you for any amount," she said.

"Oh, it wasn't the money," Cade said in a bitter tone. "I turned him down on that, so he came back with an offer I couldn't reject."

"What?" she asked, hurting all over with old wounds and fresh new ones.

"Leave it to your dad to figure out how to get to me. I was inexperienced in so many ways, Katherine. We both were."

"What else?" she asked, puzzled and reeling from Cade's revelations.

"Your dad raised the amount of money he offered, but that wasn't what got me. He offered to save my brother."

"How?" she asked.

"My oldest brother, Luke, was in jail, facing trial for robbery and assault because he got into a fight with a night watchman when he and two other guys were trying to break into a store and steal some bikes. Luke had been in trouble once before so he was facing prison. With all of his influence and contacts, your father saw to it that he could get the charges against my brother dropped by the people involved."

"No!" she cried. "My dad would never do that. He was enraged with you disappearing like you did."

"That was a damned act, Katherine. What would you expect him to do—admit what he'd done?"

"I don't believe you," she said stiffly, unable to accept that her father would do something so underhanded to one of his children.

"It's the truth," Cade insisted. "I made a promise I was never to tell you, but I'm breaking it right now. If I walked out on you without a word and left the state with my family, all charges against my brother would be dropped."

"Then you couldn't refuse him," she observed, dazed and hurting.

"In addition to helping us get along, your father agreed to give me half a million dollars. I wasn't going through with a marriage that would only hurt you in the future and at the same time see my brother go to prison when I could have kept him out. On top of all that were the nagging doubts about whether you even loved me or if you were marrying out of rebellion. How long would that last?"

He crossed the room in two quick strides and held her upper arms tightly. "Put all that together and what would you have done?" he demanded. "And then when I couldn't stand to be away from you and couldn't bear to think how I'd hurt you, and I called you—you wouldn't take my calls. Or answer my letters."

"I just don't believe my father would hurt me that way," she said, staring at Cade, wondering what had really happened.

"I don't know whether he would admit the truth if you asked him. I doubt if he would."

"I called Nick and Matt this morning to tell them you've hired me to paint your murals," she said, thinking about her father. "Matt's going to tell Dad. My dad couldn't have done anything that cruel to me, Cade," she repeated.

"Ask him, Katherine. You know your own father."

"I will ask him."

"If he denies it, he's lying. Why would I make all this up now?"

She wondered the same thing. "I'm ready to get back to Fort Worth."

He nodded. "All right, but before we leave here, let's step across the hall and you look at the rooms I have for a studio and office for you here. You can tell me what else you would like to have in them."

With stormy emotions, she followed him across the hall and entered a room that had a glass-and-iron desk, oak cabinets, a computer center with a copier, a fax machine and other electronic gadgetry. Sunshine spilled into the room from the floor-to-ceiling windows and from broad skylights in the ceiling.

"Your studio is here," he said, walking through a doorway into the next room. She entered a room that held a drawing board, easels, supplies of all types, a worktable and file cabinets. There was a large sink for her use with paints and an adjoining bathroom.

"It's great," she said, barely seeing any of it, seething over all he had disclosed and doubting him more by the minute. She expected her father to deny everything and if he did, she would believe him.

She couldn't imagine why Cade would lie to her about the past or that he expected her to accept what he said without confronting her father, but it was impossible to think her father had destroyed her future marriage.

Cade stood in the center of the room and looked around. "You can talk to my architect, tell him what you want and it'll be top priority."

"Thanks," she said stiffly.

"Ready to go? No tour of my house?"

"Let's tour another day. I want to get back and talk to Dad."

"If you're going to see him, Katherine, I'd like to be present," Cade said as they walked along the wide upstairs hallway and descended the stairs.

"Why do you want to be there?"

"I want to hear what he says and I broke a promise to him. I want to give him his money back. I don't want one damn dime from your dad."

"If he denies your accusations, Cade, and it's your word against his, I'll believe him," she said, but was uncertain if she really would, because her father would go to all sorts of lengths to get what he wanted sometimes. Except she had never thought he would with his children. They all clashed with him, particularly the years they were growing up, but he had never done anything as cruel and terrible as Cade accused him of doing. At least, nothing she had known about.

Shaken and worried, she was silent until they reached the first-floor hallway. "Our mother walked out when we were young. She fell in love with someone else."

"Maybe you ought to check that out," Cade stated solemnly.

"No. I'm sure Dad told us the truth there. He raised us

alone and sometimes he was harsh and did things we didn't like and meddled in our lives when we were older. The only one who didn't clash with him often was my brother Jeff."

"He died mountain climbing, didn't he? I read about him."

"Yes. He was wild and spoiled and Dad let him have and do most anything he wanted. They didn't go head-to-head like Dad did with Matt. Matt is more like my father, and they had some terrible battles, but Dad never did anything to hurt any of us badly, except…" she said and her voice trailed away. "I just can't believe it," she said, more to herself than to Cade.

"Except what?" Cade asked.

"He tried to buy off Olivia so she wouldn't marry Matt," Katherine replied, hurting and beginning to accept Cade's story more. "I have to hear him say that he did that to me," she said.

Cade shrugged. "Frankly, I expect him to deny it. If he does, then it comes down to his word against mine and my family. Plus the half-million-dollar deposit that I put into accounts in California banks when we went out there. Where else would we have gotten that amount?"

She stiffened, thinking things through again. "You're telling me the truth," she declared. She knew Cade's family was poor and his mother went from one menial job to another. "My father caused you to go," she said, remembering how kind her father had been to her and how furious he had been toward Cade. "He's always been strong-willed and wanted his way, but I just can't believe he would hurt me like that."

"Katherine, don't you understand—he thought he was saving you. He told me how I would ruin your life and your promising future. He was trying to protect you."

"That was my choice, and I wanted to marry you."

"That doesn't answer why you wouldn't even take my calls."

"I was so furious with you. I didn't want to talk to you again."

"You should have known that I was calling to give you my side."

"At the time after walking out on me, I didn't really care. There was nothing you could have said that would have smoothed things over. If you'd told me all you just did and every word was true—or worse—I wouldn't have wanted to get back together. Some hurts are too deep, Cade. But now, I want to hear him admit what he did."

"We'll go back." When they reached the front door, Cade held it open and as she passed him, she saw the muscle working in his jaw.

She rubbed her forehead. "How will we ever work together?"

He placed his hand lightly on her shoulder. "Easily. We've gotten through this and we're still speaking. My house is big, and we'll have a professional, working arrangement. We'll do all right. Maybe I'll fly back to California and stay away and you'll have the place to yourself."

When they climbed into the car, thunder boomed, and Cade pulled his cell phone from his pocket. "I'll call my pilot about the weather. He told me when we landed we might have a storm this afternoon, but then it should clear off in time for us to get back to Fort Worth I didn't expect to return this soon, so I didn't give the weather much thought."

Katherine was silent, her thoughts going back to her father, while Cade talked on the phone about the weather. When he finished, he turned to her. "There's a storm blowing in and it's not the best time to leave. We haven't had lunch anyway, so I'll take you to lunch and then we'll see if we can get out. How's that?"

"Fine," she replied, not really hungry, her emotions churning after Cade's revelations and her nerves raw from his kiss that she knew she would never forget.

He switched on the engine to drive away. Before they made the turn, she glanced over her shoulder and was amazed to think that in a few more days she would be living in his mansion. And her life may have changed there this morning because if what Cade said were true, she had a feeling that things would never be the same between her and her father.

Cade drove her to a small Italian restaurant and by the time he turned into the lot, a driving rain changed to hail. Cade pulled beneath an overhang. "Wait a minute," he said, switching off the car engine. "When this lets up a little, I'll take you to the door."

Unbuckling her seat belt, she turned to face him, while he did the same, facing her and stretching one long arm across the car seat. The pounding hail changed to a downpour and she felt closed into a tiny world with only Cade.

He played with a lock of her hair and the faint tugs pulled against her scalp. "I like your hair down."

"I can imagine what it looks like," she remarked dryly.

He moved his hand to draw circles on her knee with his index finger. "So what do you want out of life?" he asked her.

"To be a success," she answered instantly.

"You're already that," Cade said.

"Not like I want. I'll have to admit, Dad always fostered competitiveness in us—not in Jeff, but between Matt and Nick. I was the little sister, so I always tried to keep up, too. I think we all feel like we're competing with Dad."

"Damn. Your father—"

"Taught us how to achieve goals. There's some good in that."

"So how do you define success for you?"

"I want to open branch offices in five more cities, and with your murals, I'll have the finances. I want to get better at what I do and gain a bigger clientele for my murals. Frankly, I want a bigger income than Matt or Nick. Or at least as big."

"So do you know how much you're aiming to earn? Do you even know what they make?" he asked with amusement, and she smiled as she shook her head.

"No, I don't, but I'll know when they begin to take me seriously."

"I'd think your ten-million-dollar fee would make both of them take you seriously. Your dad, too."

"Maybe it has. My brothers sounded impressed."

"Money is cold comfort, Katherine. It can buy only so much."

"That's a peculiar thing to hear you say after the way you grew up and the money you've earned," she said. "You know what it means to be without it and you know what it means to have it."

"Money and success are fabulous, but they don't take the place of family."

"I'm surprised you feel that way," she said, staring at him and wondering how he could say such a thing with the background he'd had. "I'm amazed your income isn't your top priority in life."

"I'm astonished you don't place family first. You're close to yours."

"I love my family," she said, "but success is the most important thing in my life."

"So what are you afraid of in life, Katherine? I mean the big things, not thunderstorms and mice. What scares you? You can't even imagine being poor, so it isn't that."

She thought a moment. "Failure. I hate failing at something I try. I'm not afraid of being poor because I don't even relate to that. I guess that's what drives you and what you fear."

"No. I've lived with poverty and beaten it. Of course, it's influenced my life and it's why I like big houses and fancy cars and luxury and a pantry stocked with food."

"How many cars do you own?"

He grinned. "I have cars everywhere I go. I have a warehouse of antique and special cars. About fifty."

"You're afraid of poverty or you wouldn't collect all those cars," she said. "What else? Is there anything else in the world you fear?"

"Being alone all my life," he answered solemnly and quickly. "That would be the worst."

Startled by his answer, she gazed up at him. "Then I'm surprised you aren't married with a batch of kids. That would be insurance against being alone the rest of your life."

"I haven't found the right woman and while I want a family, I want a woman I love and like. Not just someone to fill a void. So what about you? What's the real reason why you aren't married?" he asked, watching her intently.

"I got hurt too badly when you left," she admitted. "I'll never go through that again. I won't trust anyone enough to fall in love and let someone break my heart a second time. I want my career and I want success more, anyway."

He leaned closer and tilted her head up, holding her chin in his fingers. Rain pounded on the car and they were enclosed in their own steamy space. She was aware of the closeness, of his dark eyes and his tempting mouth.

"What a waste, Katherine," he said softly. "You're beautiful, loving and passionate. You were meant for living life fully and giving to others and having children, not for boardrooms and long hours of work and balance sheets. It's an incredible waste," he said.

"It's what I want," she answered, taking a deep breath and drawing herself up as she jerked her head out of his hand. "What do you want, Cade?"

"A family," he replied instantly.

"What a thing for you to say you want when you ran away from the chance to have children."

"I never expected to earn a fortune until after I had worked for Edwin Talcott. Those first years in California, I put making money as my main goal, but I could stop work now and never lift a hand again and be wealthy. What's the point in driving to make more now?"

"I can't imagine that I'll ever feel that way, but I want the acknowledgments that come with success. I want my father's respect and my brothers' respect."

"I think you have always had that and their love."

She looked away, knowing she wanted to dazzle them with her business success. "I think you and I are poles apart—more than when we were young. It doesn't matter now. Our priorities are vastly different," she said.

"When you've finished this job, we'll go our own ways so it doesn't matter."

"If you want a family, that should be the easiest thing in the world for you to acquire. You're handsome, wealthy, sexy, charming," she admitted to him.

"Thank you. I feel that you're keeping the other half of your opinion to yourself. There's a 'but' in there somewhere."

"There should be droves of women willing to become Mrs. Cade Logan," she said, ignoring his last remark, "and equally willing to give you children," she added.

"Marriage hasn't come close to happening. When I went to California, I was busy surviving, learning, taking care of my brothers and helping Mom. Then I was occupied with business, scrambling to make a fortune and learning how to deal with it. Also, I've never found anyone I loved except you."

"Well, that was long ago and over for both of us," she declared, ignoring a flutter stirred by his statement. "There are too many bad moments and hurts between us. What's left between us is lust and I'm not interested."

"Do you ever just let down and have a good time?" he asked.

"Yes, but no thanks if that's an offer to sleep with you."

"Please give me credit for being slightly more subtle than that."

She rubbed a window and peered out. "I think the rain has let up a lot."

"Then we'll go inside," he said, sliding back behind the wheel. He drove her to the door and reached across her to open her door to let her out. She could see midnight glints in his black hair and his clean-shaven jaw. His arm brushed against her middle, and his head was only inches in front of her. He looked into her eyes.

Her heart skipped a beat as she was held, unable to move or look away. He was so close, his mouth only inches from hers. "Cade, leave me alone," she whispered without realizing it until his eyes narrowed.

"I'm not even touching you," he said in a rasp.

"You don't have to and you know it. I'm susceptible, dammit. Don't push me."

"Katherine, there's no way I'm 'pushing' you now. And I don't know how you can be very susceptible when you're brimming with wrath."

"Move out of my way," she said, her words breathless and her pulse racing. He released the open door and leaned away. The minute he moved, she slid out of the car and hurried into the restaurant without looking back. She heard the door slam and the engine roar as he pulled away to park.

When she stepped inside the restaurant to wait for him, she was breathing hard. She walked around the entrance, looking at pictures of Naples on the walls without really seeing them as she tried to regain her composure. Then Cade came through the door and her pulse escalated again.

They sat in a corner booth at a wooden table covered with a red-and-white-checkered tablecloth, then they both ordered penne and bread sticks.

"Now, shall we try a truce?" he asked as he ate.

"Of course, Cade," she replied with far more poise than she felt.

"To get on safer ground, let's discuss your office. What would you like in it?"

"I think you've covered everything in the way of furniture and lighting and electronic equipment. I'll have my laptop and I'll move one of my computers there. I want my own computers that already have the software I need."

He nodded and became silent and they ate in a quiet tension that set her nerves on edge even more. All that Cade had revealed spun in her thoughts repeatedly and each time she considered whether her father had bought off Cade or not, she had a sinking feeling that he had done exactly that.

She had little appetite and soon she glanced over her shoulder at the front windows. "I think it stopped raining completely. Call and see if we can fly out now."

"I don't have to call. I know we can if the storm has passed. I'll call my pilot and tell him we're on our way."

In less than an hour they were airborne, flying back to Fort Worth. She called and told her father that she wanted to come see him and he agreed with a cheerful tone of voice. Next she told him that she had Cade with her.

When she put away her cell phone, she glanced up to find Cade watching her. "I couldn't keep from hearing you," he said. "He doesn't want to see me, does he?"

"No, but he will. I'll take you with me unless you'd rather not go."

"I'll go. I told you that I want to give him back his money. I have it ready here on the plane."

"You're carrying that kind of cash?"

"I have a check. I intended to see him and get it back to him sometime this weekend. I don't expect him to welcome me. Far from it."

"His health hasn't been good in the last couple of years. Whatever he's done, he's still my father and I don't want to upset him," she said.

"I don't intend to disturb him," Cade replied. "I'm just going to give him a check for half a million dollars—exactly what he gave me that night."

"Where was I?"

"At home. He had me meet him at the Millington in a private room."

"You know seeing him will be troublesome," she said tightly.

"Sorry, but I want to pay the money back myself."

She shook her head, wishing the whole encounter could be avoided, yet she had to ask her father. "I'm in denial about what you told me, but if you're paying him back half a million, then it has to be true. I just can't completely accept it."

"Sorry. My intention wasn't ever to hurt you. But until you knew the truth, you'd never forgive me."

She stared at him, wondering if they could get past how they had hurt each other years ago.

They rode quietly, yet Cade sat across from her, his legs stretched out with only a breath of space between their legs, enough room to avoid touching, yet too close to forget how easily she could touch him.

"Tell me about your family, Katherine. I see Nick occasionally."

"He's married now and busier than ever and business is growing. He thrives on it just as I do. Matt is the one who stayed on the ranch and took over for Dad. Matt has his own house there and he's married. Last January they had a little boy they named Jeff."

"For your brother. That's great, Katherine. So you're an aunt."

"Yes," she said. "I've kept Jeff occasionally and, naturally, I think he's adorable. I even have his picture," she said, fishing it out of her purse to see Cade giving her a sardonic look.

"What?" she asked.

"You—whose main goal in life is success—are carrying your baby nephew's picture."

"I love my family. I never said I didn't. I just don't expect to marry and have a family of my own."

"Uh-huh," he said doubtfully as he took the picture of little Jeff. "Cute baby," he said and handed back the photo.

"What about your family?" she asked, mostly to keep from thinking about seeing her father, a moment she dreaded.

"I have a house near L.A., and so do all of us. We live in our own compound so we see each other often. I built a house there for Mom. I have a condo In L.A., as well."

Katherine remembered his mother as a plain woman who looked older than her years. The boys must have inherited their looks from their father, not their mother, Katherine thought.

"Mom's having the time of her life and I'm glad. All of us take care of her and she's found hobbies she likes and she runs on the beach every morning." He fished out his billfold and he leaned forward, his knees touching Katherine's and she drew a deep breath.

He pulled a picture out of his billfold and placed it in front of her. "Here we all are," he said. "Here's Luke, the oldest, then Micah's next and Quinn's the youngest."

She looked at four handsome men, all of them except Cade with pretty women at their sides. The only single man in the picture was Cade. He pulled out another picture. "Here's Mom."

"This is your mother?" Katherine asked in surprise. She studied a picture of a woman she didn't recognize. "She's changed completely," she said, amazed by the transformation. "She looks younger and she's very attractive," Katherine said.

"Thanks," he said, putting away his pictures. "She's had her hair styled and got contact lenses and had her teeth fixed. Little things that make a difference. She works out every day. She did the best she could for us."

Katherine marveled again at the changes in Cade and his family. "What do your brothers do?"

"They work for me. I sent them to college and two majored in finance, Micah majored in marketing and now he has a two-year-old boy."

"So you're an uncle now."

"Yes, I am. We all get together on holidays and as much as we can."

"Good, Cade. I'm glad things worked out for you and your

family," she said. "My family gets together twice a month if we possibly can." She was quiet for a long time and then looked around to see him watching her.

"You're worried, aren't you?" he asked.

"Yes. I hate to upset Dad now that his health isn't good."

"Then let it drop."

She shook her head. "No. I have a right to know if he did what you say."

"He did it, Katherine, and all the denials in the world won't change the truth."

She clamped her lips closed and turned to look out the window. Her trepidation increased with every passing hour and by the time she was finally in her father's house she was tense, dreading seeing him. Too aware of Cade by her side with a check in his pocket, she strode down the wide hall. The door stood open to the family room where she knew her father would be waiting.

"Last chance to escape," she said to Cade outside the door, and he shook his head.

"No. I want this meeting. I've waited nine years for it, Katherine."

Six

As she entered the room, Katherine called hello. Standing, Duke Ransome smiled until his gaze went past her. His face flushed and he scowled.

"Katherine, I recall telling you to come alone."

"I wanted to see you, Mr. Ransome," Cade replied easily before she could answer. He passed her to face her father. Neither man offered to shake hands.

"Katherine, you should leave," Duke snapped while watching Cade.

"I want to stay," she said and received a deeper scowl.

Duke turned to Cade. "I thought I had an agreement with you that we wouldn't ever see you again. Since you're here, I take it that you've broken your promise and you've told everything to Katherine."

Her insides knotted because in that moment, she knew absolutely that Cade had told her the truth. Her father had caused Cade to walk out on her and then misled her about it.

Hurting, she wanted to scream at her father, but it was over and nothing would ever undo the past, so she clamped her mouth shut. She was chilled, lightheaded, even though she wasn't given to fainting. Her own father had caused her heartbreak. She hurt all over because she felt betrayed, first by Cade and now by her father.

Cade withdrew his check. "I'm paying you back, Mr. Ransome," Cade said. "Here's a check to you for five hundred thousand dollars. Paid in full," Cade said grimly. "I used it well and through the investments you allowed me to make, I'm where I am today. Actually, I owe you a debt of gratitude for enabling me to achieve financial success." Cade tossed the check on a chair.

"How can you stand there and be so polite!" Katherine cried, finally unable to hold her emotions in check. She clenched her fists and shook. "Dad, how could you have hurt and deceived me the way you did?" Before he could answer, she turned to Cade. "And how can you so politely pay him back when he tore up our lives and our futures?"

Cade shrugged. "It's the truth, Katherine. I'm where I am today because of your father and his money. Absolutely and directly," he said emphatically to Duke, whose face was flushed and his fists were clenched.

"Damn you! You always were trouble—we had a deal," Duke said to Cade.

"Yes, sir, we did, but I'm breaking my promise to never return to Texas. In preventing me from marrying your daughter, you got what you wanted and now you have your money back. Don't mess with me, Mr. Ransome. I can buy out everything you own," Cade said quietly. "Katherine has agreed to paint some murals for me. You have a very talented, successful daughter and I guess Katherine owes some of her success to you, too." Cade turned to her. "Katherine, I'll wait out in the car. I'm through in here."

Cade left and closed the door behind him, and she faced her father. "How could you have done that to me?"

"I did it for your benefit," Duke answered. "If Cade had stayed here, he would never have been what he is now."

"Dad, I'll never understand how you could have hurt me like you did."

"Always remember I did it for you. Cade was trash. He wouldn't have amounted to anything if he had stayed right here. His brother was going to prison. None of us knew he would turn out like he did."

"He wasn't trash," she said stiffly.

"Don't go to work for him. You'll fall in love again and get hurt again because he's out for revenge."

"If he'd wanted revenge, would he have given you all the money back?"

"He probably enjoyed every moment of paying me the money," Duke snapped, his voice filled with disgust.

She didn't want to hear any more about it and she turned, hurrying out of the room, hearing her father calling her name, but she kept going. Not once nine years ago had it occurred to her that her father might have been the reason for Cade's disappearance. At the time she had known her father hadn't approved of him, but she'd thought he had accepted her pending marriage.

She stepped outside to see Cade leaning against the car, his feet crossed at his ankles while he waited. As he watched her approach, she forgot some of her anger and hurt.

"Let's go get some dinner," he said, draping his arm across her shoulders.

"I can't eat," she replied.

"Maybe you can by the time we get back to Fort Worth." He pulled out his cell phone, called a number and made dinner reservations.

"I'll take you to a quiet place, and we can have the evening out that I bid on."

"We had that last night," she said as he opened the door on the passenger side of the car, but he blocked her from sitting inside.

"We've gotten a lot of things out in the open since last night," he said. "We can do the evening over and this time maybe it'll be better."

"I thought it was good last night," she replied, and his chest expanded as he inhaled.

"It'll be better tonight, Katherine. You'll see," he said with his voice lowering a notch, getting that husky rasp that made her tingle.

"Cade, keep your distance. I'm still reeling from all I've learned."

"I know you are," he replied gently, "but there's no reason to sit home alone stewing over it. C'mon. One evening, that'll be better than last night," he reminded her. "That's easy."

He made it sound easy, but she knew there was a tangled history that would always be a cloud and there was the constant hot attraction that could explode into complications in their lives.

"Come on. One evening. You'll eat somewhere."

"Arm twister," she said with a sigh, knowing he was right. If she were alone, she would hurt more, let her anger ferment, and dwell on all that she'd learned today.

When she nodded, Cade stepped aside and she slid into the car.

"I know he thought he was doing it for me, but it hurts so badly," she whispered and Cade squeezed her shoulder lightly.

"Sorry."

When they drove back to Fort Worth, to her surprise, Cade stopped at his hotel. "Come up while I change. I'm taking you to a restaurant where I'll need to wear a coat and tie."

"Another visit to your hotel room," she teased.

"It'll be as harmless and uneventful as last time unless you want otherwise."

"Uh-uh. And what happens if you want otherwise?"

"Wait and see," he said with a gleam in his eye, and she smiled.

Inside the hotel lobby they took the elevator to the top floor. At Cade's suite, he held the door to let her go inside ahead of him. "I'll be right back," he said. "Make yourself comfortable."

She strolled to the balcony and pulled on the door, thinking she would go outside and enjoy the view. Turning the lock and pulling, she remembered opening the door last night.

"The door sticks," he called, striding out of the bedroom and crossing the room. He had yanked off his knit shirt and wore only his slacks as he pulled on a white dress shirt. His muscled chest was well-defined. When she looked at him, her mouth went dry and her pulse jumped. She couldn't keep her gaze from roaming all over him. She remembered caressing that chest, pouring kisses over him.

"I meant to call housekeeping and have them fix that door, but I forgot," he said.

She barely heard him, standing breathless as he jiggled the door and gave it a yank. It came open and he turned. "There you are—" He bit off his words and she looked up, realizing how she was staring at his chest.

"You remember," he whispered, catching both her hands and placing them on his chest. He was thicker, more filled out than when he was younger, and he was more muscled. He still had a washboard stomach. He was rock hard, his skin smooth, his body warm, too enticing.

She yanked her hands away as if he had placed them against burning coals. "No, Cade!"

"Why not?" he demanded. He tangled his hand in her hair and tilted her head back to give him access to her mouth. "You remember touching me," he said softly. "Why not now? Why do you want to avoid touching me? You have plenty of times in the past."

"I told you the things I want us to avoid," she whispered.

"I know what I don't want to avoid. I want your kisses and I want your hands on me now," he said. "When you look at me like that, you set me on fire. You may not know it, but your eyes are expressive and the look you're giving me ought to make me break out in flames. There's no way I can just walk away and ignore you. Put your hands on my chest."

"No!" she whispered. The word was as weak as a sigh. She looked into his dark eyes, which added to her pounding pulse. "Let me go, Cade. I told you—"

Her words were smothered by his kiss when he placed his mouth on hers. His tongue slid into her mouth, stroking, stirring fires and making her want him. Desire burst into a blaze and her hands flew to his chest to push, but then when she touched him, once again, she was hopelessly lost to passion.

Her hands drifted across his sculpted chest, feeling the flat male nipples, tracing over his powerful shoulders and then down to his strong, muscled stomach. Her hand strayed down his side, then along his thigh, before inching up to his chest again. She tore her mouth away from his. "No! Cade, we're not—"

"Yes, we are. You want me to," he whispered and kissed her, his mouth coming down hard and his tongue going deep, and all her protests ended. Her hands drifted over his chest and slid around his waist to his smooth, muscled back. She didn't notice when he pushed away her suit coat, but she felt his fingers on her blouse and then it fell on the floor beside her. Her lacy bra went next and she was pressed against his bare chest, memories taunting her, taking her back to hours of passion with him.

Trembling and torn between caution and need, she kissed him.

It was Cade in her arms, out of her dreams into her embrace and kissing her. Hunger for his caresses absorbed her. She wanted to touch and kiss him. Tangling her tongue with his, she moaned. When she thrust her hips against him, she felt his hard erection.

"No!" she gasped, pulling away. "Cade, we're different people now with different aims in life and we can't pick up where we left off," she exclaimed while her heart thudded. His heavy-lidded gaze was hot while he looked at her breasts and cupped them in his hands. When his thumbs circled her nipples, she cried out.

He leaned down, taking her breast in his mouth, his teeth nipping lightly at her nipple and then his tongue circled her taut bud.

Bombarded by sensations, she clung to his shoulders. Desire was ablaze and she moved her hips, wanting him inside her.

His hands tugged up her skirt and slid along her thighs and his fingers slipped inside her lacy thong to rub her.

Crying out, she wound her fingers in his hair as need heightened and she knew in another minute she would be over the brink. She pulled him up, her hand sliding over his thick rod, but then she pushed against his chest and leaned away. Holding his wrists, she gazed up at him. "We can't do this. No."

"We can, Katherine," he argued. "There's no reason not to when we both want to touch and kiss and love."

"There are a million reasons," she cried. "You've given me one heartbreak. Don't give me two!" She slithered into her blouse, wadded up her bra and stuffed it into her purse and then hurried to pick up her suit jacket.

When she turned, he was watching her. "What are you afraid of?"

"I just told you—heartbreak a second time. I wasn't sure I'd survive the first one. I know I don't want to have another one," she replied.

"This time we don't have to make any commitment."

"That isn't reassuring. If we make love, then I'm committed, Cade. My heart will be in it and I don't want that. We're not going back. There are too many hurts, too much has happened in the past."

"Dammit, the past is over."

"No, it's not. And the last hour brought it back to life. You're looking for a family. Look somewhere else," she snapped.

He looked at her so intently, her heart thudded and she wondered what he was thinking. Then he yanked up his shirt and spun away, but not before his glance had raked over her again.

The minute his door closed behind him, she let out her breath. How could she work for him?

Strolling to a mirror, she combed her hair with her fingers and peered at her image. Her mouth was red, her face was flushed and her hair was a tangle. She did what she could to straighten her clothing and comb her hair, letting it fall freely over her shoulders.

She ached with wanting him and kept reassuring herself that her desire was only lust.

Deciding that she could take a cab home now and have peace and quiet, she crossed the room and opened the door to the hall.

"Katherine, wait," Cade said.

When she turned around, her heart skipped a few beats. In his charcoal suit and white shirt and tie, he was incredibly handsome and it took strong willpower to keep from walking into his arms.

"Don't go without me. C'mon, we'll have a pleasant dinner," he said.

Unable to resist him, she paused. "You look handsome," she said, thinking what an understatement that was. He took her breath and dazzled her. And undressed, he did even more.

"Thank you," he said. "Ready to go?"

She nodded and they left, riding the elevator in silence.

Cade drove them to a supper club that was quiet, with soft lights, a piano bar and a small dance floor. The piano player sang as he played and Cade and Katherine were given a table that was in a secluded, cozy corner.

When she ordered a glass of red wine and the waiter disappeared, Cade's eyebrow arched. "So tonight you'll try the wine."

She shrugged. "It sounds more inviting. More than a cup of coffee or a glass of iced tea. Cade, when we finish eating, if you'd like, we can go by my office and I can show you the murals I've done. I never do the same thing twice, so at least you'll know what you can't have, but I can find out what sort of picture you prefer."

"Sure," he said. "After we dance. I paid five hundred thousand dollars for an evening with you—which you've made very clear that I had my dance last night. I think I might be entitled to at least five dances with you—that would be paying one hundred thousand dollars per dance. That's not unreasonable, is it?" he asked matter-of-factly, but his eyes twinkled, and she had to laugh and shake her head.

"Cade, I'll dance with you as much as you want. For what you're paying me, I'm willing to do a great deal to please you."

"Are you now? I recall not very long ago you emphatically refusing to please me."

"There's a limit. Dancing with you is on the 'will do' list."

"So what's on the 'will not do' list?"

"Making love."

"Let me get this straight," he said, leaning close and running his hand over hers and then taking her hand to hold it while he rubbed her knuckles with his thumb. "Dancing is 'will do'?"

"That's right."

"How about kissing?" he said, looking at her mouth and she realized she had walked into flirting and a sexy conversation with him that was already making her tingle.

"Kisses on the mouth are 'will do.' Anything beyond that, 'will not do.'"

"I think I'll stop asking and find out by trial and error."

"Right," she said, smiling at him. "You're doing something right now."

"Just holding your hand," he said in great innocence. "That's nothing. It's a great evening and I'm with a gorgeous blonde so why not hold hands and dance and kiss?"

"Remember, we're out in public."

"I can remedy that at any time. My hotel is only five minutes away."

"No. Stop flirting, Cade."

"I can't with you. You're irresistible. While we wait for our dinners, let's dance," he said, standing and tugging lightly on her hand.

She walked to the dance floor and as they began to dance, her heart drummed. How right it felt to be in his arms! She danced with him, their legs brushing, their thighs together, her hand in his.

"You used to laugh a lot," he said softly to her.

"Life isn't as easy as it was then," she answered. "And now, between us, there's very little reason for laughter."

"Relax, Katherine. There's plenty of reason for smiles between us. We're on better terms than we were this time last night. You know what happened in the past and I know why you wouldn't take my calls or answer my letters. We can move on." He smiled at her and her heart skipped. "For starters," he said, "tell me how you started in business."

"It's difficult to carry on a friendly, inconsequential conversation when I'm still in shock. The hurt and anger isn't far away."

"Give it your best shot," he said quietly, his breath warm on her temple. They moved in perfect unison and she knew there was no faulting their dancing.

"Come on. Tell me how you got started," he urged, tightening his arm around her waist and pulling her closely against him while they slow-danced and barely moved.

"I'm sure at some point I told you that I took art all through high school and I've painted murals since my junior year, but back then, it was mostly murals in my friends' bedrooms. Occasionally, someone's mother would hire me to paint a mural in a utility room or a nursery. Then in college I painted some murals on buildings and began to get more jobs. I was into computers and I put the two together. I worked in advertising and did internships. I went to work for an ad agency, but I moonlighted and before long, my moonlighting was earning more than my regular job so I quit and went on my own and the rest is history."

"And you said that there's been no one man in your life since nine years ago."

"No, there hasn't been," she said, slanting him a look. "Does that make you feel better?"

"Infinitely," he answered, and they both smiled.

"And no one seriously in your life in all that time," she said. "I don't believe it, so don't even say it."

"I was telling the truth. No commitments by either of us. Think that means anything?"

"It means we're busy and we're particular," she replied lightly. "Or—"

"There is no 'or.' Forget that."

"You've changed in the intervening years," he said. "You're more beautiful, you're more serious."

"Of course, I have. The world is different. You've certainly changed."

"How?" he asked, leaning back slightly to watch her as she answered him.

"You're self-assured now. You're sophisticated. You're better looking."

"Thank you," he said with a slight nod as he gazed intently

at her. Dancing in his arms and looking into his dark eyes sent her pulse galloping. Desire simmered constantly and it took only the slightest touch or look to heat her. They stayed in one place, their feet barely moving, while they looked at each other and she couldn't take her gaze away. He was all that she had said and more, still the most appealing man she had ever known. She hungered for his kisses that could turn her inside out and always stirred her more than any other man's kisses ever had.

Was she being foolish in guarding her heart and refusing to go back into a relationship with him?

He pulled her close and leaned his head down. "I want you," he whispered and her heart thudded.

She pulled away to look up at him. "That doesn't go with your payment. We've already settled the issue."

"Of course not. Not for one second did I think I was buying sleeping with you," he said bluntly. "This is different and what I would feel if you weren't going to work for me. It has nothing to do with your painting."

She looked up at him, for one fleeting moment wondering about letting down the barriers around her heart, trusting him again. "Old hurts would always be there between us and a chance to hurt each other again," she said.

He gazed down at her and she couldn't guess from his expression what his reaction was. "I think I can let go of the past more easily than you can. I can put it aside completely."

"Then you're fortunate," she said. The music ended and she walked back to their table with him and sat facing him. "At least my father won't meddle in my life now."

"He can't where I'm concerned, but your father is a meddler and he won't change."

Their crab and lobster dinners were left only half-eaten when they had cups of coffee poured. After a few more minutes Cade stood and took her hand. "How about my third dance?"

On the dance floor he held her close against him and they danced to a slow ballad. "This is good, Katherine. So damn good. I like having you in my arms."

"Cade, everything in you is aimed at seduction."

"No, Katherine. When I'm aimed at seduction," he said softly, "you'll know it. I'm just making a comment now."

"Right," she said, shaking her head at him. "Let's put getting personal on the 'will not do' list," she said lightly, hoping she could keep the evening light and impersonal.

"Let's not," he replied. "I like slow-dancing. I like getting personal with you. I like kissing you—"

"Cade," she said in exasperation, leaning back to look up at him, and he gazed down at her with a crooked smile.

"All right. Impersonal. What mural have you painted that you like the best?"

"Actually, the one I enjoyed the most was a mountain scene in a lodge in Colorado. I loved the place and I liked doing the mural. Speaking of murals, if we're going by my office, we should go soon."

"We can go now. I'll claim my remaining dances another time," he said easily, taking her hand as they left the dance floor.

Another time ran through her thoughts. How long could she resist him? How much would she see him in the future? She suspected a lot.

It took only a few minutes to get to Ransome Design on the tenth floor in the Renaissance Building. She switched on lights as she entered her corner office and turned to find him looking around.

"Nice, Katherine," he said and she glanced at her office that had an antique mahogany desk, an elegant mahogany table with chairs around it, comfortable upholstered chairs, bookshelves, oil paintings on the walls and tall potted plants.

"There's a bar," she said, motioning toward double doors. "I'll get the books with the murals," she said, reaching up to a high shelf. As she started to pull out books, Cade's arm stretched overhead and he grasped the books.

"Tell me which ones and I'll get them," he said, taking down books for her. He had shed his coat and as soon as they had the books, he shed his tie and unbuttoned the top button of his shirt. Turning away, she slipped out of her suit coat and glanced around to find him watching her. She drew a quick breath and met his gaze.

"You're not wearing anything under that silk blouse," he said in a husky voice.

"Cade—"

"Here are your books," he said, his voice still low. Her office was warm, slightly stuffy, and she didn't want to pull on her suit coat and it seemed ridiculous to, but she also didn't want to stir Cade's desire. Dismissing it, she sat down at the table and opened a book.

"Pull up a chair," she instructed, trying to sound all business. "What I'd like to do is get the presentation for the first mural, get your approval and start painting. Then there'll be times I can work up ideas for the second one. That way we can start sooner, and I can concentrate on one mural at a time."

"Sounds like a good plan to me," he agreed.

He sat beside her and they looked through books while he made comments. Taking notes, she was aware of brushing their hands together, more faint touches that fanned fires. Soon, she realized he was going to be easy to please because he liked most everything she showed him.

Losing track of time, she finally had enough ideas to make suggestions and sketches that she thought she might work up into a proposal for him.

To her surprise, he picked out what he liked. He leaned close as she sketched out a drawing of an outdoor scene from a balcony that would look like an extension of the room. Beyond the balcony, land stretched away with a European flair in the beds of flowers, trees and in the distance a stream with a bridge.

"I'll draw and paint this scene. Pick at least two more for me to paint and present to you so you have a choice."

"No need to. I like this and you know exactly what I like," he said, his tone changing, and she forgot the drawing to look at him.

"Are you going to flirt constantly?" she asked.

"Every time I can," he replied.

His shoulder and arm touched hers and he was close beside her. He ran his finger along her jaw. "You don't need to do this one up in a sketch for me. I can tell from the drawing you've done that that's what I'd like to start with in the dining room."

"Then I'll do it for myself so I can see how it'll look. You're easy, Cade," she said, breathlessly, thinking about him more than the mural.

"Too bad you're not easy," he whispered, drawing his index finger lightly around the curve of her ear and creating tingles.

"So we're set and I can move in and start drawing?" she asked.

"As soon as you can," he replied. All the time they talked, they gazed into each other's eyes.

She tried to think clearly, looked away and struggled to get her mind back on the matter at hand. "I guess I can move in by next Tuesday."

"Monday we'll go to your bank," he said.

"I'll have to wind up things here Monday, too."

"I'll get an appointment at the bank for us. Where do you bank?"

When she told him, he nodded. She pushed back her chair and stood. The room had closed in and was hot and she needed to get space between them before she did something foolish.

"Just leave the books here. I'll put them away later," she said.

As he smiled and gathered them up, she shrugged and picked up her suit jacket.

Instantly, he set the books down on the table and reached out to take her arm and draw him to her. "Before you put on that coat," he said, pulling her close. "Come here, Katherine," he said in a husky voice.

Desire flashed in his dark eyes and her pulse jumped.

"Cade—"

He slid his arms around her and leaned down to kiss her in the manner that always stopped her protests.

His mouth covered hers and her heart thudded as his tongue went deep into her mouth. She wound her arms around his neck. One kiss fluttered through her mind and then all thoughts were gone. She was lost in a magic world of his kiss that awakened every nerve and fanned the flames she already struggled to keep under control.

She wasn't aware of him tugging her blouse out of her skirt, but she was conscious of his hands sliding over her bare skin and caressing her breast, rubbing his palm over her nipple in a delicious friction that made her thrust her hips against him.

"Cade—" she repeated his name and his mouth covered hers, possessive and demanding and she moved against him, feeling his thick rod. He was hard and ready for her, wanting her.

Her skirt fell away and he held her hips, leaning back to look at her, making her tremble. She wore only her thigh-high hose and her thong and his hot gaze raked over her like a caress.

"You're so damn gorgeous…" he whispered and pulled her to him, leaning over her as he kissed her, bending down so she would mold against him and cling to him. She felt his crisp white shirt, warm because of his body, his soft wool trousers and belt buckle pressing against her.

His hands slid over her bare bottom and along the back of her thighs and then his hand went between her legs, slipping beneath her thong to stroke her. She held him, moving her hips, moaning with craving for more of him as her hand slid down to his trousers and she rubbed his hard shaft.

With a sob she pushed against him. He straightened and she stepped away.

"We're not going to make love!" she cried. "You're not going to seduce me!" With shaking hands she yanked up her clothes, feeling his hot gaze pouring over her as she grabbed her skirt and stepped into it, and yanked on her blouse.

Gasping for breath she turned to face him. "You're not getting my heart the second time. We'll hurt each other again," she cried. He stood in a wrinkled shirt with half the tail hanging out over his waist. His erection pressed against his wool trousers. Cade's face was flushed and he was gasping for breath as much as she and in spite of doing what she thought was the wise course of action, part of her wanted back in his arms to kiss and love him.

"I never ever wanted to hurt you," he said, grinding out the words in a husky voice. "Not then, not now."

"Don't even say that! Back then, when you left, you may have thought it was best for my future, but you knew you were hurting me and you did it to save your brother."

"So I should have stepped back and let him go to prison?" Cade snapped.

"No, of course not. I didn't mean that. You did what you had to do, but you knew you were hurting me. And we're poles apart now with different lives and lifestyles."

"We've been over this," he said and she clamped her mouth shut.

She pulled on her suit coat as if it were armor, tugging it closed over her breasts. Her blouse was only partially buttoned, the tail of it hanging out of her skirt, but she didn't care. "I'm ready to go."

He crossed the room and walked beside her without touching her. She switched off the lights, glancing at her worktable and wondering how long it would be before she could look at that table and not see Cade standing beside it, disheveled, aroused, wanting to make love.

They returned to the car and rode in silence while she tried to regain her composure. And beneath it all, desire was a scalding flame, hotter than ever.

At her house, he stood facing her. "You let me know when you'll be ready to move and I'll send movers to get your things."

"I won't have that much," she said, shaking her head. "I can get my things in my car."

"Pack enough to last. Six murals will take a while."

She nodded. "I'm glad you told me what happened," she said quietly, and he nodded.

"I know it's put a rift between you and your dad."

"I'd rather know. In a way it was the most important time in my life. Rift or not, the truth is best."

"I'm glad you think so," he said, looking intently at her. The moment drew out and she knew if she didn't move, she might be back in his embrace.

"Good night," she said and stepped inside, closing the door quickly behind her without looking back.

She let out a long sigh as she walked to her room. The events of the day ran through her mind, but the predominant images and memories were of standing in Cade's arms in her office while he kissed and caressed her.

She was moving to his house Tuesday. How would her heart survive the challenge of being with him?

Seven

As Cade strode down the hall to the dining room of his mansion, he slowed and walked more quietly. It was Thursday and over a week ago on Tuesday, Katherine had moved into his Houston home. Last Thursday morning he'd had to fly to California. It had been one week that seemed as if he had been away from her for a month. His eagerness to see her increased with every step he took.

Pausing in the open doorway, he looked inside. Scaffolding was along one wall. The furniture had been moved to one end of the room and draped with cloths as an extra precaution to keep paint off. Drop cloths were spread on the floor beneath the scaffolding and ladders. Katherine stood on a platform as she drew on the wall.

When his gaze flicked over her, his pulse jumped. She was in a T-shirt and cutoffs and had one thick braid that hung down her back. Taking his time, he looked down her long, shapely legs, and then up over her round bottom, mentally peeling away her cutoffs.

With his pulse racing, he leaned one shoulder against the doorjamb and continued to look at her. She had always set him on fire and she could now more than ever. She was more beautiful than she had been when she was twenty. He thought about her kisses when they had been in her office. Just memories aroused him.

He liked watching her work. It fascinated him how swiftly she drew and her certainty in what she was doing. He had come back to Texas with an opposing mix of emotions, wanting to see her, hoping to hire her, but still steaming over her refusal to answer his calls and letters. And then when he saw her at the auction, she had taken his breath away with her beauty and he wanted her more than he ever had. He'd had no intention of getting involved emotionally with her again because of their stormy history, but now that was fading and accusations were in the open and reasons clarified.

Cade watched her draw. With the past put behind them, the big barrier of her damnable drive and ambition and craving for success remained. He didn't want to fall in love with a woman who was bound heart and soul to her career. He didn't want that in his life. But he wanted Katherine in his bed. She made his blood boil, and he wasn't sleeping nights because of thinking about her and wanting her. Never had he known a woman he desired the way he did her. And he hadn't met any who could kiss or make love like Katie. She was beautiful, sexy and off-limits.

He remembered their kisses in her office and knew she wasn't totally off-limits. She couldn't resist passion, either. His gaze roamed over her with speculation. He wanted her in his bed. And soon.

Trying to get his mind back to other things and cool down, he thought about the evening. He had something to tell her and he debated whether he should or keep everything to himself. As always when he had such a decision to make, he viewed it from whether or not he would want to know if it were he who was in the dark. Good or bad, he'd want to hear it.

She glanced over her shoulder, saw him and paused. "I didn't hear you."

"I didn't intend to startle you."

"You didn't."

"I'm enjoying the view."

She wrinkled her nose at him. He wanted to go get her down off the platform and kiss her, but he knew she wouldn't want him to. Dropping his navy suit coat and navy tie on a chair, he strolled across the room. Halting near her, he put his hands on his hips and looked up at her drawing.

"How long have you been standing there?" she asked.

"Not long. It's fascinating. Absolutely gorgeous," he said, stepping closer to the foot of a ladder. His gaze drifted over her legs again. "Perfect," he said.

"You're not talking about my art work."

"No, I'm not," he said. "I'm standing here drooling over the view. Come down here."

"I don't think so," she said lightly. "If I did, that might be the end of my work today and I'm getting things done."

"We can get things done together," he responded and she smiled.

"Seduction? I can get more drawing finished. I'm not climbing down."

"If I didn't think we'd fall off the platform, I'd come get you, but ladders, I take seriously. Of course, getting to kiss you, I take rather earnestly, too."

"You keep your feet on the floor," she said. "Kisses aren't part of this deal as I have to continually remind you."

"As if you didn't enjoy them, too," he reminded her while she turned back to continue her sketching.

He watched her sure strokes. "It doesn't scare you to just start drawing on my wall?" he asked.

"No. I've done this a lot and drawing on your wall is exactly what you paid me to do," she said, going back to her drawing.

"Looks like you're making a lot of progress. You're fast, Katherine."

"Why do I feel you've been telling me that since we first met?"

He grinned. "Come down here and say that," he coaxed in a husky voice.

"Not on your life," she snapped.

"Want to take a break?"

She glanced at her watch. "I can't believe it's half past five. I thought it was about three. I didn't realize it was so late."

"Even though it's October, it's a warm, humid day. The pool will be great. Want to join me?"

She shook her head. "I'll keep drawing."

"Scared to swim with me?" he asked.

"Don't try to goad me into it. I'm going to continue drawing."

"I'm leaving again tomorrow afternoon to fly to back to California. I'll be gone until next week. Think you can get along without me?" he asked, and when she glanced over her shoulder at him, she smiled.

"I'll manage, Cade. When you're gone, it's very quiet and I can get a lot done."

"So I'm dismissed." He turned away, picking up his coat and tie. "I can take a hint," he said over his shoulder and left to go to his room and change for a swim.

Later he heated the grill and began to cook shrimp kabobs. They sizzled on the grill when he heard her approach. Turning to watch her, his pulse jumped.

She had combed her hair out, catching it behind her head with a blue ribbon, and she wore a pale blue cotton blouse, blue skirt and sandals and she looked beautiful.

Putting down the spatula he held, he gave her his full attention. He crossed the patio to place his hands on her shoulders. When her big blue eyes focused on him, he wanted to wrap his arms around her and kiss her.

"You look as gorgeous as ever," he said quietly instead. "And you smell delectable, too."

"Thank you. You don't look so bad yourself," she replied lightly.

"I'm almost ready to put everything on the table."

"So where is Creighton?" she asked.

"Gone. I gave all of them the night off. We have the house to ourselves and I'm cooking."

"I don't know whether that's good or bad—your cooking, that is. Having the house to ourselves is tempting fate."

He smiled. "So you'll admit that I'm temptation," he drawled.

"You know your answer. You've been temptation since you pulled alongside my pickup that afternoon. Now my dinner may burn, so you better see about it."

"Yeah, I'm hungry, too," he said.

The cool evening was pleasant and Cade enjoyed her company and relished even more just looking at her.

It wasn't until they finished eating that he stood and walked around to her side of the table, pulling up a chair to sit close, facing her. "I want to talk to you."

With a questioning arch of her eyebrows, she waited while he placed his elbows on his knees and leaned closer. For a second he forgot what he intended. He studied her, thinking he could look at her for hours. Her skin was smooth and flawless and her full red lips were enticing, while her big blue eyes and rosy cheeks added to her beauty. Longing to touch her, he kept his hands to himself.

"I have something to tell you," he said, trying to break the news as gently as possible and wondering again if he were doing the right thing or not, but he was committed now.

She frowned slightly. "I have the feeling that you're going to tell me something I don't want to hear and you're getting me braced for it. My family's all right, isn't it?"

"Of course. Sorry, I didn't mean to frighten you about them," he said, squeezing her shoulder lightly and then letting his hand linger, wanting to let it drift down to her soft, full breast. Instead, he gazed into her eyes and tried to focus on what he was telling her. "As far as I know you family is fine, and that isn't what's on my mind at all."

"I didn't really think it was because you would've told me about them immediately. What is it? Just tell me."

"Long ago you told me about your mother walking out on all of you."

As Katherine drew a sharp breath, her breasts thrust against the cotton blouse and he couldn't keep from looking. "I'm not certain I want to hear this," she said.

"That's up to you, but I thought I ought to give you the choice. I know what happened to her. If you don't want to know, I'll drop it now and never bring it up again. It'll hurt to hear," he warned her.

Rubbing Katie's shoulder lightly, he waited. He didn't want to hurt her, but he thought that she, as well as her brothers, had a right to know. Why one of them hadn't checked into it, he couldn't imagine, except they had probably grown up convinced of Duke Ransome's lies about their mother.

Katherine gazed at him and, in spite of the tense moment, longing for her rocked him again. He always thought of her as Katie, not Katherine, and it was an effort for him to remember to address her by her full name. He turned a lock of her hair around his index finger and could remember running his hands through her silky hair.

"Tell me," she said finally.

"Did you know she had an affair with another man?"

"That's what I heard when I was grown. Growing up, I didn't

know anything except that she left us and was never coming back. We were always told she didn't want to see any of us."

Cade moved closer and let his knee touch Katherine's lightly. "Your father found out about the other man and was so enraged that he sent her packing and told her to never come back."

"No! He said she didn't want to have anything to do with us or him."

"Maybe with him, but not with her children."

"No, no!" Katherine exclaimed. Closing her eyes, she put her head in her hands. "All those years—our mother—" She raised her head. "Did she marry the other man?"

"No. It was a short affair. You father threatened her if she ever tried to contact any of you in any way. She believed him and she's stayed out of your lives, but she's in Houston."

"Houston!" Katherine exclaimed. "All the years we were growing up she's been here in Texas?"

"Yes, but it's part way across the state," he said, avoiding telling her that her mother had kept up with all of them and gone to see them when she knew they would be out where she could observe them without them seeing her.

"Cade, I don't know my dad at all," Katherine said, looking stricken. "How could he do that to his own children?"

"She had an affair and your dad is an unforgiving man. He's a hard man. He's strong-willed. You know he gets angry when he doesn't get his way."

"To separate us from her all that time. We should have been able to see her occasionally!"

"I agree, Katherine, and I'm sorry. My father died when I was young and I was angry over losing him and hurt for years. In a way, what happened with your mother is worse because it could've been avoided."

"Olivia has asked me about her twice and she's talked to Julia. They urged us to look up our mother, but Matt, Nick and I didn't want to because Dad drummed it into us when we were little, that she left and didn't want any part of us ever. That's painful."

"I'm sure it is."

"It hurts to discover my Dad has such a dark side. I knew he did things to other people, but I didn't think he would be so cruel to his own family. All those years he deceived us."

"Let's get something straight here," Cade said firmly. "You brought it up about your mother. I felt like you had a right to know the truth if you wanted to hear it. I didn't tell you to be vindictive toward your father. I don't hate your father, Katherine," Cade said solemnly. "It wasn't what he intended, but he helped lift my family and me out of the gutter. He kept my brother out of prison. He gave us the money that I used to start investing. We were dirt poor and we knew how to live on nothing, so we took that money and made the best possible uses of it we could. At the time, I hated your dad, but after about four years, that hatred had diminished to dislike. I'll never like him, but I don't hate him and I don't feel any need for revenge. I meant what I said when I told him that I owed him gratitude for what he did for us."

"I'm glad you told me about our mother. I have to let the others know," she said. "I'm close to Nick and Matt. I told both of them what he did to us."

"Did they believe you?"

"Oh, yes. They've had more run-ins with our dad than I ever had. They weren't surprised. They were surprised you paid him back. Especially Nick. Nick has a vindictive streak, but I think it's mellowed since he met Julia."

"I don't want his money now."

"Cade, have you talked to my mother?"

"Yes. If you want to meet her, you can. All of you can," he said, sliding his hand to Katherine's nape, knowing she wasn't even aware of his touch. He couldn't resist touching her and, right now, when he looked at her full lips, he thought about how incredibly soft they were, how they burned him like fire.

"Yes, I'd like to meet her and I imagine Nick and Matt will, too. Especially after they learn the truth. How did you find out all this?"

"It wasn't hard. I guessed that none of you have ever tried to look her up."

"No, we haven't," Katherine said with a twinge of guilt. "Olivia thought we should try to find out and hear her side of the story. Olivia's not overly fond of Dad, but then he tried to buy her off, too."

"The bribe worked for me because of my brother. He must not have had anything else to hold over Olivia's head."

"No, he didn't, I'm sure. You said it was easy to find my mother. How come you even looked?"

Cade leaned forward to place his hands on his knees. "I was going to come back here to build this house and when I decided that I wanted you to do the murals, I hired a P.I. to check into things here. I wanted him to let me know about you and your family. It came up about your mother and I told him to check that out, too, because it pays to know as much as you can. When I found out about her and that she was in Houston, I was curious enough to go see her myself and I had a long, interesting visit with her."

"What's she like?" Katherine asked.

"She's a beautiful woman. She went back to school and got a law degree. She paints, too. She was friendly to me."

"Has any female ever been unfriendly to you?" Katherine asked, and he grinned. "I want to meet her," Katherine said. "How long have you known about her?" she asked, tilting her head to study him.

"I found out several months before I came to Houston to pick out a lot for my house. It was sometime last year."

"Last year! Why didn't you tell me that first night? It's my mother."

"That didn't seem to be the time. And later, you were shocked to learn what your father did to us. I didn't want to break it to you right then on top of everything else you had just learned about."

"So you just kept it all bottled up," she said. "What else have you kept quiet about concerning me?"

"No more family secrets. The only thing I've kept from you is telling you how much I want you in my bed," he said, unable to keep his voice from thickening. Her big, blue eyes widened as she focused on him and he looked at her full, sensuous mouth that was made for kisses. He leaned forward to pick her up and place her in his lap.

She struggled and his arm tightened around her waist while he kissed her neck behind her ear. "Be still. I've been gone since last week and all I could think about was you."

"Cade, don't turn on that seductive charm of yours," she said, wriggling to get off his lap.

He wanted her and he knew how to end her protests. He shifted slightly, tightened his arm and kissed her. The minute his mouth covered hers, he was aroused. He tucked her against his shoulder as he leaned over her to kiss her long and hard.

She struggled for a second, pushing against his chest while she wiggled, but then her arm slid around his neck and she turned against him, pressing against his chest while they kissed.

His pulse roared and he shook with a hunger that wasn't going to be satisfied until he made love to her for hours. She was ready for loving, coming apart now in his arms as she shook and moaned softly and kissed him back with enough passion to burn his mouth.

As if he could kiss away her damnable drive for success, he leaned over her and kissed her as passionately as he possibly could. His hand slid down her throat, caressing her lightly, slowly, and then going lower, down over her breast. His fingers twisted free buttons and in seconds his hand was beneath her blouse, unfastening her lacy bra. He cupped her breast in his hand. Soft and warm, she was irresistible.

He ached with wanting her, leaning over her and letting his hand slide down her length and then back up under her skirt. Her skin was smooth. She was all curves and softness and fire.

He framed her face with his hands. "I want you," he said, the words a rasp while his heart pounded and he looked into her blue eyes, that were heavy-lidded now with passion. Her red lips were swollen from his kisses and her hair fell over her shoulders, the ribbon lost. "I want you, Katherine, and you'll be mine. I want to make love to you for hours."

"No! Cade, we're not complicating our lives that way again," she protested, but she was breathless and he could feel her racing pulse and desire burned in her eyes in spite of her words.

"You want to love. You kiss like each time is your last," he whispered, kissing her throat and stroking her. He shook with desire, burning to peel her out of her clothes and kiss her all over. There had never been anyone who set him on fire like she did. He had never been able to get her out of his mind and now that he was with her again it was as if the years between never existed.

He raised his head to look into her eyes. "I'd swap all my millions to be that poor kid on my bike and have you making love to me and letting me make love to you again."

"We can't go back—"

"We don't have to go back when it comes to loving," he whispered, kissing her and stopping all her conversation. She had stiffened when she had protested, but now with his kiss, she lost her resistance and molded against him, her hand sliding down to caress him and he groaned with pleasure.

He raised his head. "I'm going to kiss you and love you until you forget all about that business you crave more than anything else. I can make you forget it," he declared, and his mouth covered whatever she had been about to reply. He held her tightly, and then turned her on his lap to straddle him, giving him access to her so he could slide his finger into her panties and fondle her while he kissed her.

She moaned and twisted and moved on him, driving him wild in turn. He ached to possess her, but he knew she wasn't going to let him yet.

He groaned again, her hands were on him and she was tugging away his belt. Her skirt was full and he shoved it out of his way and yanked off her blouse and bra as he kissed her.

He cupped her breasts, relishing her softness that filled his hand, so incredibly soft and curvy. Sliding down to her tiny waist his hands moved over her, and then one went back beneath her panties to stroke her while he slid his other hand over her bottom and back to her nipple.

He rubbed her, a friction that made her move her hips. When he pleasured her, she set him on fire with her responses. He was rock hard, feeling as if he would burst with need, aching and wanting her softness to envelope him.

"I want inside you, darlin'," he whispered. "I want to take you and make you mine and love you for hours," he said until her mouth covered his and she kissed away his words. He shifted and placed her on the chaise that was at hand and then moved between her legs, leaning down to put his tongue on her intimately where his hand had been. With her knees hooked over his shoulders, he watched her, wanting to drive her to a frenzy.

"No!" she cried emphatically, pushing against him, wriggling and scooting away to stand. Her skirt fell in place, but not before he got a view that burned him like a brand. Every inch of her was gorgeous. He gasped for breath and could hear her raspy breathing as she looked around and grabbed her blouse to yank it on.

"Cade, we're not doing this," she said.

He wondered if she had the remotest idea had badly he wanted her and how beautiful she looked to him right now. She was disheveled, her silky blond hair spilling over her shoulders. Her skirt was a mass of wrinkles and her blouse was open as she began to button it. Her lips were red from his kisses. In the throes of passion he had made declarations of desire and told her how he wanted her and he had meant everything he said, but he doubted if she heard or would remember any of it.

"We're not going to become lovers! That's not part of the deal," she snapped.

"I want you. And that isn't part of any deal. It's just a man telling a woman that he desires her."

"There's no future for us," she said fastening the last button and jamming her blouse beneath her skirt. "None. We're worlds apart. You want a family. I want my career unencumbered by a family. End of conversation." Her head came up. "End of lovemaking. That ought to be clear enough." Stepping off the chaise, he walked toward her. Her eyes widened and she edged away from him.

"Do you hear me?" she asked, taking another step back.

"I hear you perfectly clearly," he answered calmly. "I know what I want—I've always known. How long did it take me to settle on what I wanted for the first mural?"

She had backed up to the brick wall that circled one side of the patio. He put his hands out on either side of her to block her in.

"Move out of my way," she said breathlessly and sounding as if she didn't possibly mean it.

"I know what I want and I go after what I want and often I get what I want," he said quietly. "What a waste, Katherine, for you to give priority to an office over a home and family. You don't even want both like many women do."

Her big blue eyes gazed up at him and snapped with fire, but her lips were parted and he suspected she was only half-angry with him, while the other half of her wanted him.

"I'm not changing any more than you are."

"That doesn't mean we can't make love. You want to and I want to."

Something flickered in the depths of her eyes while she shook her head. "No. I can't be casual about loving or go into it knowing it's temporary and inconsequential. That's impossible. I don't want the entanglement."

He was hard, aroused, and he wanted her. But he didn't want to send her off and spend the evening alone. He wanted her company. He jerked his head.

"Sit down. I'll get us cold drinks and let's see if we can let the dust settle and calm down and just talk. C'mon, Katherine. Talking isn't anything."

"It is with you," she said in a small voice that made him draw a quick breath.

He fought the impulse to reach for her again because of her remark. Instead, he turned away. "Sit down. What would you like to drink? How about some pop?"

"Fine. I want to call my brothers and tell them about our mother. Cade, you know her. Would you call her tonight and tell her I'd like to meet her and talk to her."

"Sure. You'll find she's easy to talk to," he said. He pulled out his wallet and retrieved the slip of paper with her phone number and got out his cell phone to call.

When Laura Ransome answered, he talked softly, and in a minute turned to Katherine. "She said why don't you come see her tonight. We're in the same city."

"Now?" Katherine asked, her eyes going wide.

"Sure. I'll take you. You can go in and see her without me." Katherine nodded and he made arrangements. When he broke the connection, he glanced at her. "I told her we're leaving now."

"No, we're not! Let me change and comb my hair," she said, rushing inside. He watched her hurry away, knowing while all three younger Ransomes would probably be happy to find their mother, Duke Ransome would be an enemy forever after tonight. Cade didn't care. There wasn't anything Duke could do to him any longer.

He left to get ready himself to go and then returned to the patio to wait for Katherine, who appeared in minutes.

He glanced over her plain black dress that ended above her knees and hugged her hips. Her hair was swept to one side of her head and pinned, and she took his breath away.

"You clean up right nice, Miss Ransome," he said, and she smiled.

"Thank you. Cade," she said, grasping his arm. "I feel all fluttery and nervous," she said. He was aware of her clinging to him, so uncustomary for Katherine. He draped his arm across her shoulders and squeezed lightly.

"You'll be fine and you'll like her, Katherine, and then you can tell your brothers."

They hurried to his car and he drove to the residential area to a redbrick house nestled in tall pines.

"I can wait in the car so you two can be alone."

"Don't you do it," Katherine said. "You know her. You come with me. Please, Cade."

"Two words I never thought I'd hear," he said dryly as he got out to go around the car and open her door. He held her arm and waited beside her until the front door opened and they faced a tall, black-haired woman with huge blue eyes and still beautiful skin, and Cade knew where Katherine got her looks.

Eight

Katherine couldn't get her breath as she gazed into blue eyes that matched her own. Cade held her arm lightly.

"Mrs. Ransome, here's your daughter, Katherine."

Laura Ransome reached to take her daughter's hands, and Katherine grabbed and held tightly. Then Laura hugged her and Katherine wrapped her arms around the slender woman in return.

"I used to dream about you and imagine this moment," Katherine said.

"This is so wonderful," Laura said, releasing her. "Come inside. There's no need to stand out here."

"Katherine, if you two—"

"Come on, Cade. If it weren't for you, this wouldn't be happening." Katherine wiped away tears as she caught his hand and tugged lightly. He followed her and closed the door.

"We'll go to the back living area. That's where I spend all my time," Laura said. Katherine looked at the warm house that was beautifully furnished with oil paintings on the walls and polished wood floors and green plants in pots and vases. They entered a room that had a brick fireplace, sofas and chairs in bright upholstery, a piano in the corner and bookshelves. There were baby pictures on the shelves, along with pictures taken later, and Katherine recognized herself and her brothers. She crossed the room to a picture and picked it up, looking around in wonder at her mother. "This is my high school graduation."

"I hope you don't mind that I took your picture without you knowing about it," Laura said.

"Why didn't I see you?" Katherine wondered, staring at her mother.

"You wouldn't have known me if you'd looked right at me," Laura said gently.

Katherine replaced the picture on the shelf and saw more of herself and her brothers and she realized her mother had been in her life in a small way all through the years.

"I wish I'd known."

"We can't undo the past. Come sit and tell me about yourself."

She glanced at Cade. "Probably Cade has filled you in on a lot." Katherine sat on the sofa beside her mother and talked about her life. All the time they talked, she took in her surroundings and the woman she faced and she was equally aware of Cade sitting quietly in the wing back chair near her, his foot propped on his knee.

Laura Ransome had smooth clear skin and large luminous blue eyes that were thickly lashed. Her black hair had only a few strands of gray, and when she smiled or laughed she had a dimple in one cheek and even, white teeth.

Katherine liked her instantly and tried to avoid thinking about the lost years. All she could do was pick up and go on from here and be profoundly thankful that Cade had searched for her mother and then had told her about Laura.

Once she glanced around at Cade. "Bored with all this talk

about the Ransomes' early years?" she asked him, and he shook his head, smiling at her.

"Of course not. Go ahead and talk. I like hearing about the Ransomes," he said easily.

"I can imagine," Katherine said, smiling at him and turning back to Laura.

Katherine tilted her head to one side. "What do I call you?"

"Whatever you like. It's Mom, Katherine. Mother is fine. Ma—that's okay, too. If you're more comfortable with Laura, I can understand."

Katherine laughed. "Mom. I can't believe it, Mom. My mother, Mom." The two looked at each other and both reached out at the same time to hug.

When the hour grew later, Laura got them mugs of hot chocolate and they sat around the kitchen table, sipping the chocolate while Katherine told her more about herself and her brothers and fished pictures from her purse to show Laura.

When it was nearly midnight, Cade took Katherine's arm. "It's late, Katherine. We should go. You two can see each other again soon."

"I didn't realize," Katherine exclaimed, standing. "I'm sorry to have kept you so late."

"I loved every minute and I stay up until after midnight anyway," Laura said, standing and walking to the door with them.

"We'll all get together. I'll call Matt and Nick tomorrow and you'll probably hear from them, too." At the door she turned to face her mother. "My mother. I can't believe it after dreaming about this moment all the years I was growing up."

"Oh, Katherine," Laura exclaimed and wrapped her arms around Katherine. Katherine held Laura, joy filling her to finally find her mother.

They separated and said goodbyes and then Cade slipped his arm around Katherine as they walked to his car.

Laura stood on the porch, waving and watching them drive away. As soon as they rounded the corner out of sight, Katherine threw her arms around Cade's neck and hugged him tightly.

"Hey!" he said, pulling to the curb and stopping instantly. "You'll make us have a wreck," he said, laughing.

"Thank you, Cade," she said, on her knees with her arms around his neck. "Thank you for finding her, for telling me and for going with me tonight. Thank you, thank you!"

"Katherine, can you save all this gratitude and show me when we get home?"

She laughed and kissed his cheek and he caught her around the waist and hauled her onto his lap, cramming her between the steering wheel and him while he kissed her hard. Startled for an instant, she was immobile and then desire flashed white-hot with his kiss and she wrapped her arms around his neck to kiss him until his hands fumbled for her zipper. She sat up abruptly and moved away.

"We're out in public in your car!" she exclaimed, scooting back on the passenger side.

"You started it," he said, breathing hard and looking at her intently.

She waved her hand at him. "Just drive us home. I'll calm down and I just wanted to thank you."

"Any chance of getting that thank-you from you again at home?"

"Absolutely none," she answered with amusement. "Well, maybe a little, but not the kind of gratitude you have in mind."

"Why am I not surprised?"

She laughed. "Cade, I'm so happy to find her and she's all I dreamed about."

"You don't know that. You've only been with her a few hours."

"It's the second time you've been with her and you liked her and don't rain on my parade."

"I wouldn't think of it. She does seem great," he said

solemnly. "I'm glad you're happy because I've worried about telling you. It was sort of damned if you do and damned if you don't."

"You've made an enemy forever of my dad," she said solemnly. "He's not a good person to cross, Cade."

"He can't hurt me, and I don't give a damn."

"I'm so glad you told me. So, so, so glad."

"You just hold that thought," he said.

She placed her hand on his knee and his head whipped around. She patted his knee and smiled at him. "Pay attention to your driving. I'm just about to explode with happiness."

"I wish I could make you that happy."

"You have tonight."

"No. For different reasons."

"You've made me even happier in the past and you know it," she said solemnly, removing her hand.

"Don't lose all that joy," he said. "I'm glad for you and for her, Katherine. She was thrilled and happy to meet you. She seems like a great person."

"Cade, she's beautiful. How could Dad have done that?"

"Just an angry man whose ego blinded him."

"I'm not worrying about what Dad has done. I can't undo any of it and at least now, I know about him and know what happened and I've found my mother. I'm calling Nick right now."

"It's after midnight."

"He won't mind." She got out the phone and glanced at Cade, who seemed to be concentrating on his driving and she put away her phone. After a few minutes, Cade looked around.

"I thought you were calling your brother."

"You've spent the evening listening to me talk about growing up and telling my mother about Matt and Nick and Jeff. Now you don't have to sit and listen to me telling Nick what I've been doing."

"Call him. I'd rather you call him right now. I might get another hug of gratitude when we get home."

When we get home. The words sizzled in her each time he said them. How right it seemed in so many ways, and he couldn't ever guess how grateful she was to him for what he had done in finding their mother.

She called Nick and told him and then had to tell Julia and answer questions. Finally she was off the phone. "It's too late tonight to call Matt. I'll call him in the morning. Nick said you did what he should have done a long time ago. Each time he and Matt talked about it, they decided to leave it alone. All of us were told that she never wanted to see us again and we just grew up believing Dad about it. Nick said he should have guessed it might not be the truth. He's surprised that Matt accepted it all these years."

"Well, you know now," Cade said, pulling into an open garage. As soon as they were in the house and he had locked the door he turned to face her.

"Now, Katherine, come here and thank me."

Katherine's pulse jumped as she faced him. Closing the distance between them, she wound her arms around his neck again.

"Thank you," she said, gazing into his dark eyes and smiling at him. "You're wonderful!"

He wrapped his arms around her waist tightly. "I want to make you this bubbly and happy and hear you say that to me for another reason."

"I can't," she replied solemnly. "There are too many things in the way. Face it, you want sleeping together without commitment and, ultimately, you want a wife and family, children. I can't do either."

"You mean you don't want to," he said, his dark eyes clouding and a muscle working in his jaw.

"I'm married already to my job. And I don't have time for

children. I don't have time for a husband. Now, that said, for tonight—thank you. I'm so grateful for what you did. It's the most wonderful thing you could possibly do!" She wrapped her arms tightly around his neck, pulled his head down and kissed him.

His arms tightened around her waist and he leaned over her and kissed her. Her heart thudded while she gave herself over to kissing him.

His kiss deepened, plundered her mouth. Again, he framed her face with his hands. "I want you and you'll be mine, Katherine. I want that joy for life and your exuberance."

"I can't give you what you want, Cade. This is lust and you want to make love and that'll satisfy you, but it won't me. I'm way too complicated to simplify it down to that. So, no, I can't meet those terms. But I am grateful beyond measure to you for tonight."

She walked away from him, her pulse racing from his kiss. She was aware he watched her with his dark eyes heated by desire.

"Maybe soon we can all get together. Come with me, Cade. I want you there," she urged, turning to face him across the kitchen.

"All right, I will. In the meantime, it's a warm night and you're too excited to sleep. Let's swim and then we can have a glass of wine."

"That sounds like a plan for seduction."

"Come on, Katherine. You're not going to sleep and you can always fend me off. All it takes is a no that you mean."

"If I say no, I mean no," she said, in a haughty tone, half teasing him because she was still thrilled and excited. "How about we cut the swim, have the glass of wine and just talk?"

"It's a deal. Anything to be with you," he said. He opened a bottle of red wine and poured them both glasses and got out a chunk of cheese and a box of crackers.

As she watched him, she kicked off her shoes and sat on the kitchen sofa, crossing her long legs at her ankles. He brought everything in to set it all on the fruitwood table in front of the sofa.

The minute he sat beside her, he reached out to wind her hair in his fingers. "I'm happy for you. I thought she was very nice, but I did worry and debate about telling you. I'm glad you're happy and you liked her."

"I love her, Cade. I thought it would be awkward and like a stranger, but it wasn't. And I'm glad you went with me."

A corner of his mouth quirked up. "Why? I didn't do anything."

She shrugged, looking into his dark eyes, aware of his hand playing with her hair that made slight tugs on her scalp. He was so close, sitting beside her, his hip pressed against hers.

"At first I was nervous, and it helped to have you with me."

"I'm surprised, but pleased." He handed her a glass of wine and held his up in a toast. "Here's to finding your mother."

"Oh, Cade, I'll drink to that," she said, touching his glass and watching him intently over the rim as he sipped.

He watched her, his dark eyes burning with desire that made her pulse race. She was excited, happy and she tingled beneath his steady gaze. Setting down his glass, he took hers from her. He picked her up to set her on his lap.

When he did, she wound her arms around his neck. "I thought we were going to sit and talk," she said breathlessly, promising herself just a few kisses with him and then she'd stop.

"You want me to kiss you," he whispered, showering kisses on her neck. "I can see it in your eyes." His kisses went up over her ear and then he leaned back to look at her. Her eyes were closed and her fingers played in his hair.

She opened her eyes to meet his mocking gaze before he lowered his head to kiss her.

As she clung to him to kiss him in return, her heart thudded.

His kiss spun her into a vortex of desire. From the moment she had looked up into his eyes at the auction, longing had torn at her with a hunger for his lovemaking that she had fought steadily. But need had built and Cade had fueled the flames with each encounter. She was in his arms, kissing him, and she wanted him. She had debated with herself, fought desire and finally yielded to searching her heart for what she truly wanted.

She knew her desire wasn't going to end. Now she was in his arms and no matter what the future held for them, she suspected only heartbreak again because they were on divergent paths in life, but she wanted him now.

Her pulse pounded as she wound her fingers in his hair, pressed her hips against him and kissed him, pouring all her heat and longing into the kiss. He twisted free her buttons and shoved off her blouse. Her lacy bra was gone in seconds and then he unfastened her skirt and pushed it around her hips.

As his hands roamed over her, he groaned deep in his throat, but she barely heard the sound for her roaring pulse.

"I want you!" she gasped, crying out the words as she slipped her hands over his powerful shoulders, relishing his sculpted muscles.

"You set me on fire, Katie," he whispered, and hearing him call her Katie sent another tingle spiraling in her. Time vanished and took with it painful memories and old hurts and anger. She was in Cade's arms again, loving him and she let go of everything from the past except her love for him.

Heartbreak might lie ahead, but at the moment it was a dim threat that she didn't care to acknowledge. Cade in her arms, his body hers again, hers to kiss and touch and love was all that mattered.

"You're so gorgeous, you take my breath," he whispered, his hands sliding to her waist to hold her away from him while he looked at her in a slow assessment that was hot enough to burn her to cinders. His hands followed his gaze, drifting over her shoulders and down to cup her breasts as he stroked them.

Mesmerized, she closed her eyes, tilted back her head and held his arms. He leaned forward slightly to take her nipple in his mouth and circle the taut bud slowly with his wet tongue.

"Cade," she whispered in ecstasy.

He slid his hands lower slowly, down over her ribs and she opened her eyes to find him watching her and then his gaze slipped down again as he slid his hands between her legs and rubbed her, holding her away from him to watch her when she reached for him.

"I'm going to drive you wild with desire," he whispered.

He toyed with her languidly while she gasped and cried out and squirmed to reach for him, but he held her where he could watch her.

"Come here!" she cried.

He scooped her into his arms and carried her into a downstairs bedroom to set her on her feet in front of a full-length mirror, turning her back to him as he slid his hot, hard rod between her legs. "Ride me, Katie," he ground out the command in a husky rasp. "Give me pleasure while I make you want me."

His legs pressed against hers, squeezing her against his gorged rod, that was thick and torrid between her legs. Wrapping his tanned arm around her pale waist, he held her close against his solid, naked body.

"Look at us, your beautiful body. Look how you excite me," he whispered, kissing her ear while he fondled her breasts.

He was heated, his shaft pressing against her intimately, a pressure that tantalized and drove her to new heights as she moved against him. "Cade!" she gasped, placing her head back against him and wanting to turn to kiss him, but he held her.

"Cade!" she gasped as the sizzling friction between her legs drove her. "Please—"

"Open your eyes and look at us together," he said, his voice a thick rasp. "Open them, Katie, love."

Love. The word sent tremors spilling in her.

"Look at us now," he ordered again. "Open your eyes and see what we do to each other."

Her eyes flew wide. She saw her pale body against him, his broad shoulders dark behind her, his long legs covered in short, black hairs. Their images barely registered because feelings consumed her, heightening her need for release as she moved her hips frantically.

"You're wickedly sinful, Cade," she whispered.

"Not as wickedly sinful as I intend to be before I take you and make you mine totally. I want to love you right out of your mind."

"You already are," she whispered, closing her eyes and moving her hips, holding his narrow hips while sensation escalated. She ached for him and ran her hands over his hips, trying to reach him as she twisted and writhed against him. "Cade!"

"I want to call you Katie again. I want to seduce you, make you mine in every way possible. I could devour you, I want you so badly," he whispered. His hand circled her nipple, increasing her need. "I've dreamed of you—"

A sob escaped her. He was driving her wild physically while his words were propelling her emotions to as great a need as her body. Desire was a raging fire, roaring in her veins.

With a cry she pulled away from him, turning to press his thick rod against her while she wound her arms around his neck and pulled his head down to kiss him again.

His hands slid down her back, easing over her bottom and stroking the back of her thighs while he kissed her. Their tongues tangled, stroking and going deep.

She trailed kisses along his throat and then down to his chest, her tongue circling his nipple while her hand teased his other nipple. He played with her breasts, in turn stroking her.

She knelt in front of him, her tongue flicking over his thighs, around his throbbing shaft, while he groaned and tangled his fingers in her hair and finally thrust his manhood against her mouth.

She opened her mouth to take him, sliding her lips so slowly over him, trying to build the fires in him that he had in her. Seduction went two ways and was a delight and a torment and she wanted him to feel all that she did.

"You're mine, Cade," she whispered, not expecting him to hear her. "You're mine in a way you'll never be anyone else's." Then words were gone as she drew her tongue along his shaft, licking him while her hand slid between his legs and she stroked him lightly, cupping him and touching him.

Finally she took him fully in her mouth, her tongue circling his velvet tip. Then she slid her tongue up and down the length of him, stroking and licking him slowly.

With a groan his hands slipped beneath her arms and he lifted her to her feet so he could wrap her in his arms to kiss her.

He lowered her to the floor and rolled her on her stomach, moving between her legs while he showered kisses on her nape and she curled her hands against the floor, wondering how much she could stand before she had to turn over and kiss him.

Lost in streaks of fire, she clenched her fists and tried to roll over, but he gently held her.

"Let me love and kiss you and look at you. You're beautiful, Katie," he whispered. He traced kisses down her back, over the curve of her bottom and then his warm breath was between her legs and she sobbed and bucked and tried to turn to kiss him.

"Wait, darlin'," he urged. "Let me love you long and slow until you're ready for me."

"I'm ready for you," she tried to cry out, but it came out a breathy rasp. "Cade, I want you."

"Not half as much as I want you," he replied, skimming

kisses down the back of her thigh and then his tongue was behind her knee while his hands dallied over her and one hand slid between her legs.

"Cade, now! Let me turn over."

He shifted and she rolled over while he knelt between her legs and pushed her shoulders as she started to sit up.

"Let me look at you all I want," he whispered. "And see what I can do to make you want more. Do you like me to touch you here?" he asked, his hand stroking her breasts and she closed her eyes and caught her lower lip between her teeth as she moved her hips slightly. She stroked his thick rod.

"Yes, I like it and you already know it," she gasped. Her eyes flew open.

"Cade, there hasn't been anyone else. I couldn't. Not ever," she confessed. "I wanted to because I was so hurt and angry and I went out intending to wipe out memories of you and get back at you, but I couldn't. You're the only man."

"Lord help us, Katie," he said, blinking and staring at her and then he pulled her into his embrace to kiss her with such passion that she shook in his arms and forgot what she had admitted.

"I'm going to love you all night," he said when he released her slightly. Dazed, she barely heard him as she pulled his head to her to kiss him again.

After a moment he raised his head only a fraction. "Are you protected?" he asked.

"No. I'm not," she answered. His mouth covered hers again.

She didn't know how long they caressed and kissed each other, but then he scooped her into his arms to carry her to the bed. He left, retrieving his trousers, striding back to her as he retrieved a packet.

"Hurry, Cade!" she gasped, reaching for him.

As he knelt between her legs, she watched him pull on the condom. His shaft was dark, thick and ready. And she was eager for him, locking her legs around him to tug him toward her while her hands stroked his thighs.

"Hurry. Come here and make love to me," she gasped, watching him intently.

He lowered himself to kiss her. His eyes were midnight black now with pinpoints of desire heating their darkness. His gaze raked over her before he wrapped her in his embrace and kissed her.

Her heart pounded and she arched to meet him. She felt the hot tip press against her and then ease so slowly inside her. Her cry was bitten off with his kiss.

Ecstasy enveloped her at the same time. And the knowledge that Cade was in her arms, added to her eagerness. "I've waited nine years!" she gasped, the words whispered and she suspected they were lost on him.

"I've wanted you like this. Make love to me," she cried and then kissed him again.

"Katie, love!" he gasped as he eased slowly into her until he filled her. He withdrew and plunged again, taking his time to increase her need.

Her heart thudded from his words and from his lovemaking. She thrashed wildly beneath him and her hands raked over him, clutching his firm butt to pull him closer. He moved slowly, tantalizingly, easing in and out of her in an exquisite torment that drove her to desperate need.

She moaned and cried out while her hips thrust against him. Her long legs were locked around him, holding him.

Sweat dotted his forehead now and she knew he was holding back to pleasure her.

"Let go, Cade. Lose your control!" she cried. Desire raged with a dizzying urgency.

"Want me the way I want you," he said. He ground out the words in a tight, husky voice that she barely heard.

"I do!" she cried in return.

"Katie, give me all of you, everything, your passion, your body, your heart. Put me first again in your life and allow us both another chance."

She could barely hear his raspy whisper, but she did hear the words. They meant little at the moment. Now she saw blinding lights exploding behind her closed eyelids, heard nothing except his whisper and her roaring pulse.

Her craving for him intensified. She gasped for breath and raked her hands over him, clutching him, relishing every inch of his powerful body.

"Now!" she cried, feeling a climax building toward an explosion of relief. Then release came, sending tremors that shook her.

He thrust, moving his hips even faster as he plunged deep into her softness and finally he groaned.

"Katie, Katie, love!" he cried, holding her tightly with one arm beneath her as he pumped into her and finally sagged on her and held her.

Their galloping heartbeats and ragged breathing gradually slowed to normal. He rolled on his side, keeping her with him. He combed damp strands of hair from her face with his fingers and he gazed into her eyes.

"Katie, I've dreamed of that too many nights to count. How I wanted you! I missed you, wanted to see you, fantasized about you."

She gazed at him solemnly. "I have, too, Cade."

"I should have let you know sooner. In fairness, I tried and you didn't want to know. Then I was angry and tried to let it all go, but I never could," he said, and her pulse drummed.

She ran her hands up and down his smooth back, which was damp with sweat. "That's past. Let it go and I will, too."

"I'm happy to forget it," he said showering kisses on her temple as he stroked her hair away from her face.

"Cade, we just complicated our lives horribly."

"No, we didn't," he argued, propping his head on his hand to look down at her. "Move in with me."

"Slow down. Just go slower. You want it all at once," she urged, running her hands across his powerful shoulders, and then threading her fingers in his hair.

"Damn straight, I do. If I could," he said, nuzzling her neck and then tracing the curve of her ear with his tongue, "I'd keep you naked in my arms for the next week."

She laughed and wound her fingers in his hair, looking into his dark eyes. "That's not such a bad idea—"

"Darlin', you're giving me hope!"

They gazed into each other's eyes. Satisfaction brimmed in his brown eyes and she felt it mirrored her own feelings. She wasn't thinking one minute beyond where they were and she had replied flippantly to his remark, knowing he hadn't been in earnest, either.

"This is paradise," he said, pulling her tightly in his embrace to hold her close against him. "I've dreamed of this so many nights that I couldn't possibly count them."

"So have I," she whispered, running her free hand down his back and over his bottom. She slid her fingers back up along his hip, relishing touching him even though she was satiated.

"You've filled my thoughts constantly," he said. "I don't like leaving here to go to California to work or anywhere else. I want to be here with you. I would like you all to myself, un-interrupted, nothing else going on."

"That's impossible and you know it," she said. She placed her fingers on his lips. "We're not going to argue on this night. No discussions of the past or future. Just now, Cade. We have this night and I want to enjoy it to my heart's content because I have dreamed about having it a thousand times over."

His eyes darkened and he gazed deep into hers before he kissed her again, a deep, consuming kiss that was a confirmation of intimacy and closeness. They had forged a new bond tonight and, fleetingly, she hoped that bond didn't turn into golden chains tugging at her.

He shifted away and combed her long hair from her face. "Beautiful, beautiful," he whispered, kissing her lightly.

She caressed and kissed him languidly, wrapped in his arms and in euphoria over the lovemaking that she had desired for years.

"Come shower with me," he said later. He stood, picking her up to carry her upstairs to his bathroom to his shower.

"Cade, this is the biggest shower I've ever seen, short of something for a gym," she said, looking at his huge glass-and-marble shower.

"I hope it doesn't look like a gym shower," he said without taking his gaze from her as he became aroused again. He turned on the water, running his hands over her, sliding his warm palms over her wet nipples.

She gasped with pleasure, closing her eyes and caressing him, turning to rub her bottom against his hard shaft. She was giggly, playful, happy over loving him and ignoring every caution and worry and reason to resist.

They played together beneath a warm spray of water while he seemed to enjoy her as much as she did him. Finally, after getting a condom, he lifted her, braced himself against the wall, spread his legs and slowly let her slide down onto his ready shaft. His dark eyes bore into her and then she gasped with pleasure and closed her eyes.

Her legs were locked around him while she held him and moved with him and he thrust his hips, filling her and withdrawing as hot need rekindled and blazed.

They climaxed together, his cry of her name dim over her roaring pulse. Not until her breathing and heartbeat had returned to normal did he lower her to her feet.

"I don't think I can stand alone," she said, smiling at him while she stroked his cheek.

He turned his head to kiss her hand. "You can better than I can," he said. "Let's rinse off and get back to bed."

"That means another round of lovemaking," she said and received a probing scrutiny.

"Is that bad?"

"Not for me," she replied and he flashed her a smile that almost buckled her knees.

"Don't give me one of your million-watt smiles. My knees will go," she told him as they washed and he turned off the water.

Taking the towel from her, he dried her, sliding the rough cloth over her slowly in tantalizing strokes that stirred desire again.

She dried him at the same time. "If you don't stop that, we'll be back in the shower and we'll never get out of here."

"Fine with me," he said, sliding the towel between her legs and drawing it back and forth while he watched her.

She drew a swift breath, making her chest expand and her nipples thrust toward him. He raised the towel to rub circles on her nipples and she closed her eyes as ecstasy streaked again, tingles mixing with heat inside her to increase her yearning for him.

Her hips moved and she grabbed his wrist to tug at him. "Stop," she whispered. "You're tormenting me."

"You don't like this?" he asked, kneeling down to draw the towel slowly between her legs.

"Yes," she gasped, winding her fingers in his hair as she moved her hips faster. He dropped the towel and kissed her, pulling her into his tight embrace and leaning over her and they forgot everything except passion.

It was almost dawn when he fell asleep in her arms in his big bed. She gazed around his room. A low light burned and she looked at Cade's mammoth television screen, his desk with a laptop opened on it, shelves of books that made her wonder when he had become such a reader. She looked at him, holding her close against his side with his tanned arm around her waist.

His dark lashes were black shadows on his cheeks and his jaw had a faint stubble.

As she looked at him, her heart thudded. She had always loved him and he was the only man she'd ever loved. There was no future for them, though, and she was certain he felt the same way about tomorrow that she did.

She had meant what she'd told him. She wanted her career. She was equally certain that he had been sincere when he had said that he wanted marriage and a family. It surprised her that he did, but he'd have to find them somewhere besides with her. She had no place in her life for either of those things.

She dozed and drifted into a fitful sleep with dreams of Cade.

Hours later, she stirred and opened her eyes in bright sunlight. She turned her head to see Cade's dark gaze on her.

"You know what I want?" he asked in a deep voice.

"I can well imagine," she said, running her hands over his chest as she turned on her side to face him.

"Any chance you want the same thing?" he asked, caressing her breast.

With the first feathery stroke of his fingers over her nipple, she closed her eyes. Desire burst inside her and she wanted all of him again as if they'd never spent hours making love the night before.

"Cade," she whispered, opening her eyes to look into his briefly before she cupped the back of his head, leaned closer and kissed him.

He rolled her over beneath him, keeping his weight only partially on her as he supported himself slightly and kissed her. Her pulse drummed and she wanted him with a desperation that startled her. Her hands slid over his back, his buttocks, his thighs. She couldn't get enough of his muscular, strong male body.

Kneeling between her legs, he moved lower, taking her nipple in his mouth and licking so slowly in a hot, wet torment while his hand stroked between her legs.

Desire rocked her, building with each caress and kiss.

Pushing him down, she climbed over him, slathering kisses on him and then taking his rod into her mouth until he growled. He sat up to swing her into his arms, cradling her head against his shoulder while he kissed her senseless. In minutes he moved her over him to straddle him, settling her on his stiff manhood.

She gasped with pleasure as he eased into her, filling her, driving her wild. She thrashed, going faster and faster until her climax burst and she sprawled over him while he climaxed and held her.

They settled again and finally she could breathe normally once more.

"Katie, you're amazing. And you've melted my bones. When I can stand, we'll shower—"

"No. There's no 'we'," she said, rolling over to face him. "I have work today and you do, too. I'll use my own shower and you can have yours all to yourself."

"Can I come watch?"

"No. Not this morning. If you look, we'll make love again."

"And that's bad?" he asked, looking amused, but he was watching her intently.

"That's not in today's order of events."

"Oh, damn. A plan for the day. How about kisses between your legs for the top priority instead?" he asked in a husky voice that added to seduction. He leaned closer to kiss her neck. "How about half an hour of kisses like that or my hands here," he said, circling her nipple with his thumb. "Or my hand here?" he asked, caressing her bottom.

She slid out of bed and hurried away, certain he watched her. She grabbed a towel from the floor and wrapped it around herself before looking back at him. He stood by the bed. He was naked, aroused and male perfection. One look at him and her blood heated.

"Katie, will you move in here with me?" he asked.

Nine

He stood waiting, wanting her right now with a hunger that had grown instead of diminishing.

"That's not fair, Cade, and we've discussed this," she said.

"We discussed a lot of things, but not you moving into my room. I want you in here at night. I can love you, hold you all night, and that's what I'd like. And I hope what you'd prefer," he said quietly, wanting her there more than he could remember wanting anything in a long time. She was in his blood and he didn't think he could ever get enough of her.

"Think about it," he urged, buying time because by tonight, she would be more susceptible to his touch and his caresses.

When she nodded, his pulse jumped. He watched her turn and leave the room. He wanted to go after her, but he knew he should leave her alone.

The big barrier between them was her craving for success. He didn't want to fall in love with a woman who was totally wed to her career. And he reminded himself that he damn well better remember that before he was in love with her for the second time and setting himself up for another disaster.

He swore, but then he looked back at the bed and remembered her there in his arms, and he was in flames again with wanting her.

He showered and dressed in jeans and a T-shirt. He didn't have to fly out until the afternoon, so he was staying home this morning to enjoy her company. He realized, wryly, that she might boot him out anyway. He found her in the kitchen with Creighton serving her breakfast. Two smiling faces turned toward him.

Cade spoke to both of them, barely aware of Creighton.

"Morning, Mr. Logan," Creighton said. "I'll have your breakfast right away."

Cade sat down across from her. In one swift look, he took in her cutoffs, her T-shirt and her bare legs with her feet in sneakers.

"Fine. No hurry," he said, looking into her wide blue eyes while she smiled at him and made his heartbeat quicken.

"What's your schedule?" he asked her.

"To spend the day drawing," she said. "Soon I can start painting."

He nodded. "You'll stop and take time to have lunch with me before I leave, won't you?"

"Yes," she said. He wanted to take her hand and pull her into his lap. He resisted the urge and they talked about inconsequential things, but he was aware that he wasn't alone with her. By the time they finished toast, orange juice and omelets, he couldn't remember anything they had talked about and he ached to pull her into his arms and kiss her.

After breakfast he strolled with her to the dining room. As soon as they entered the room, he closed the double doors. She turned to give him a quizzical look.

"What are you doing? Your staff might come in to clean or for some other reason."

"I feel like I haven't kissed you for a month," he said, his pulse pounding.

"Cade, I'm getting ready to work."

"I'm going to kiss you. That's a helluva lot more important," he said, sliding his arms around her waist. "You have to learn to prioritize, Katie."

"You're back to calling me Katie. I think Katie is long gone—"

He pulled her to him and kissed her, silencing her conversation. She was Katie to him always and he wanted to call her by the nickname. He leaned over her, kissing her hard, getting another rush of pleasure when her slender arms wrapped out his neck and she kissed him.

He was on fire with wanting her. Still kissing her, he saw a long table with blueprints spread on it. Cade's fingers twisted free the buttons of her cutoffs and pushed them away. He slipped his hand beneath her shirt to cup her breasts, caressing her nipple, leaning down to push away her shirt and bra and take the taut bud in his mouth. His tongue drew lazy circles around her nipple while she moaned, wound her fingers in his hair and moved her hips.

"I want you. You'll be mine, Katie," he said and then he leaned back and pulled off her T-shirt and tossed it aside, unsnapping her bra and letting it fall while he cupped both breasts and leaned down to circle her nipple with his tongue.

Her shaking hands were at his belt buckle, unfastening his belt and jeans to push them off his hips.

"Katie, love…" he said showering kisses on her. He wound his hands in her hair and tilted her face up. Her eyes opened slowly and focused on him.

"You're mine," he said, grinding out the words and then he leaned down to kiss away any protest.

As he kissed her, she peeled away his shorts and he yanked off her lacy panties. With a swoop of his arm, he sent the blueprints flying from the table.

He picked her up and placed her on the table, spreading her legs and grasping her bottom to pull her to him.

"Cade," she whispered, her hips moving, her blond hair fanned behind her head. She was beautiful and naked and open to him.

"We're not alone—" she whispered.

"Yeah, we are," he answered, leaning over her to kiss her and lifting her hips with his hands as she wrapped her legs around him. He thrust into her softness and then they were moving frantically as she cried out with pleasure.

He thrust fast, pounding in her, driving her to a swift climax, and then she took him to release. They were gasping for breath. He pulled her into his arms and she wrapped herself around him while he carried her to a chair and sat to hold her close.

"Cade, you're scandalous—"

"No, I'm not. I'm a man who desires a beautiful, sexy woman. You're temptation and fire and rapture," he whispered, brushing her hair away from her face with his fingers.

She kissed his throat. "Suppose someone knocks on the door?"

"I'll tell them to go away," he said, barely thinking about it. "Every time I make love to you, I want you more than before."

"I know," she answered solemnly, raising her head to look into his eyes. Her mouth was red and swollen from his kisses and she was naked in his lap. He let his hand drift lightly across the tips of her breasts.

She inhaled and closed her eyes for an instant. Then she looked at him. "We're like a runaway train on a track headed to disaster."

"No, we're not. You're irresistible."

"I'm getting my clothes," she said, climbing off his lap.

He knew he should, as well, and he put them on while watching her.

"I'm going up to shower again," she said, turning to him. "I may lock you out of this room."

He held up his hands as if in an act of surrender. "I have some work to do before I leave again for California."

When she nodded and hurried away, he went to his room to freshen up. Glancing at her closed door, he wondered if they were headed for disaster. Could he walk away from her again and not have his heart torn out a second time?

It was hours later as he flew over the Arizona desert and tried to concentrate on the papers spread in front of him that his thoughts went back to Katie. He didn't want to give her up. He suspected no one would ever talk her out of her drive for her career. He recalled her statements to him: *"I want my career, unencumbered by a family. End of conversation"* and *"I'm married already to my job. And I don't have time for children. I don't have time for a husband"* and *"I want my career and I want success."* Repeatedly, she had given every indication that she'd meant what she said to him—no kids or marriage for her. Her career was all-important and he might as well accept that fact.

At least for now, he wanted her in his bed every night he was in Houston, and he expected to succeed into talking her into that.

He clenched his fists and wished he were back in Texas with her. Was he falling in love with her again? Had he ever really stopped loving her? He faced the question squarely. Was he in love with her still—once and always in love. He closed his eyes and thought about life without her. He'd hated the last trip when he'd had to leave her behind.

Was what he felt really love or lust and hunger for what he'd lost in the past? They were two different people now, so did he love her?

In the nine years between leaving Texas and returning, he'd tried to forget her, he'd gone out with other women, but no one ever captured his heart except Katie. He clamped his jaw so tightly closed that it hurt. She was stubborn, determined and she'd spent a lifetime competing with her brothers and father. Cade knew she meant what she said when she declared her career came first.

Cade stared out the window and saw her big blue eyes. He loved her and he might as well decide what he was going to do about it this time. Before he had walked out on her. Was he going to have to again? Or declare his love and let her reject him? Had his exorbitant fee for her murals pushed her solidly into a life choice of her career? Or was there some way to win her love?

He opened his clenched fists. She had loved him enough in the past to plan to marry him. Could he win her love again to that extent? It was too late to run from falling in love with her. He was already deeply in love with her if he faced his feelings honestly. Now what was he going to do about it? Was there any way for them to have a future together?

Katherine drew, concentrating on her work and refusing to think about the morning or last night or kissing Cade goodbye this afternoon when he left for another short trip to California.

Cade wanted her to move into his bedroom, be in his bed every night when he was here in Houston. Was that a wise course of action for her to pursue?

She drew a line and leaned back to look at the fountain she was drawing. She studied it, climbed down and walked back to look from a distance. Satisfied, she climbed back and continued drawing, concentrating until she remembered Cade's kisses.

With a long sigh, she focused on her drawing. She wasn't going to let her heart rule her life and right now she was consumed by Cade's lovemaking. She had managed her life without him before. She could do it again, she reassured herself, but it was hollow. She already missed him. When he was gone, the mansion was big and empty. Cade's presence filled it and added excitement and vitality. She wanted him here now.

She remembered their lovemaking, his hands caressing her and his hot kisses until she was breathing hard, wanting him and aching.

She gazed out the window, but only she saw Cade's dark eyes, heard his whispers. *Katie, love.* She could hear him saying the endearment, but she reminded herself that it was in the throes of passion. She knew he wanted her, but she didn't know if he would let himself go and love her and if he did, she couldn't return his love the way he'd want her to with marriage.

She ran her hand across her forehead. She wasn't the same person as that twenty-year-old girl he'd fallen in love with long ago. She had changed and her aims in life were different now. Katie Ransome was now Katherine, so dissimilar.

Her gaze ran over the empty dining room. She knew the staff had gone to their homes and she had the mansion to herself. It was empty, lonely and no wonder Cade didn't want to spend his life alone in the mansions he must own!

She loved him. It was that simple if she were honest with herself. She loved him, always had, probably always would. There had never been another man for her that she truly loved. "I love you," she whispered in the big, empty room and looked at the dining table covered in a drop cloth. What woman would be the hostess at that table? What children would he have?

Katherine hurt. She loved him, but it didn't change one thing. She didn't want to give up her career for a husband and family. Not now, especially when she was on the brink of getting to do all she had ever dreamed about in her business. She had always planned that the next office she would open would be Houston, to be followed by Kansas City, but with Cade living in Houston, she decided to open Kansas City first and get time and space between them.

Focusing on drawing, she managed to go another half hour before her thoughts returned to Cade. He wanted her to move in with him. That would just make it more difficult later. By the time she lived with him and finished his murals, she would be so wildly in love it would be devastating to leave. At the same time, if she stayed and worked, there was no way she could resist him and stay out of his arms and out of his bed.

She bit her lip and frowned as she drew and then stepped back and looked at her lines. She erased her light pencil lines furiously and concentrated with all her effort to keep Cade out of her thoughts.

"Cade," she whispered, knowing she loved him and this job would be unavoidable heartbreak because she wasn't going to marry him.

The phone rang and she hurried to answer, wondering if Cade were calling. Her pulse jumped at the sound of his voice and she sat down on a chair by the phone. It was an hour later when he told her goodbye, promising to call her later.

Humming, she switched on lights and went back to work, working until late and pleased with how much she was getting done.

It wasn't until late that night when she lay in bed alone that she let her thoughts go back to replay every minute of the night before with Cade and she ached to be with him right now.

Last night had been rapture to make love and touch and kiss all night. To talk and laugh together. Even to just sleep together wrapped in each other's arms

Was he going to interfere in her work? Probably to a small extent. Was he going to break her heart again? She couldn't answer her own question, but she suspected he would. They had different goals in life and she couldn't see Cade changing. Nor did she care to change. His princely sum for her art had cemented her ambition.

A pang of longing tore at her when she thought of kissing

him goodbye. He'd looked into her eyes while tension pulsed between them. When he had turned and walked out, she had watched him and it had hurt to see him leave.

What would she do when he walked out for good? Or when she finished the job and told him goodbye?

Saturday morning while she was drawing, Mrs. Wilkson appeared with a phone in hand. "Ma'am, this call is for you. It's someone from the Chavin Corporation."

Katherine climbed down and took the call, crossing to a work-table to get a pen and piece of paper. A deep male voice introduced himself as Gary Tarlington with the Chavin Corporation and he wanted to meet with her to discuss murals for his business.

Friday afternoon of the following week, Cade climbed out of his car near a back entrance to his Houston home. As he strode toward the door, he thought about his decision. Katie had told him she didn't want a relationship without commitment. He knew she had declared that she didn't want any obligation because it would interfere with her career. She didn't want children, and he did. They were at an impasse, but he didn't know how strongly she really felt about it. He intended to find out because he wanted her in his life permanently. He had never forgotten her, never gotten over her, and if that wasn't love, he couldn't imagine what was.

They needed to get it all in the open and find out where they were going. He wanted her and at the same time, he wanted a family and children. He loved her, but he wasn't going to settle for a future with a wife who put her career first and who wouldn't give him children.

On edge, yet with his pulse racing over being with her, he unlocked the back door and strode into the hall. When he passed the kitchen, he stopped to say hello to Creighton, who was nowhere to be seen.

The table was set for two with crystal, candles and flowers, and he smiled, turning to stride toward the dining room, expecting to find her on the scaffolding painting the mural. He peeled off his charcoal suit coat and shed his tie, tossing them on a chair in the hall. His heels clicked on the marble floor as he strode toward the dining room.

"Cade."

He looked up the sweeping stairs. Dressed in a short, indigo dress and high-heeled sandals, Katie stood at the top of the stairs. His heart slammed against his ribs.

The moment he saw her, she smiled and started down the steps.

His heart thudded because she was beautiful. Her hair was pinned high on either side of her head and in back it fell loosely across her shoulders. Her slender hand was on the banister and she kept her gaze on his as she descended the steps.

"You look fantastic!" he said.

"Thank you. You look quite nice yourself," she said, stopping inches in front of him on the second step and wrapping her arms around his neck to kiss him.

His arms circled her waist instantly, holding her close. She was incredibly soft and sweet-smelling, and her curves crushed against him. She held him tightly while she kissed him. Aroused, his blood heated with a hunger that had built each minute he had been away from her. He wrapped his arms tightly around her, wanting to hold her and never let go. He leaned over her and kissed her in return as he reached behind her to tug down her zipper.

Her hands flew over him, caressing him, unbuttoning and unfastening and pushing away his clothing as swiftly as he peeled her out of her wisp of a dress.

"We're here alone, aren't we?" he asked.

"Yes," she said, pulling him close to kiss again until he leaned down to take her breast and stroke her nipple with his tongue.

She gasped with pleasure, caressing his thick shaft until he groaned and picked her up.

As he kissed her, she wrapped her legs around him. He spread his feet to brace himself while he lowered her on his thick manhood. Her softness and warmth enveloped him. Hot and wet, she was ready, and he moved his hips, thrusting with all the driving need that had grown in him while he had been away.

"Katie, love!" he gasped, grinding out her name before his mouth covered hers again.

Clinging tightly to him, she moved and moaned. Her hips pressed against him and his heart thudded while his pulse roared. Fire raged in him as he plunged wildly until his climax burst in a release that sent shudders through him.

She cried out, clutching him and moving frantically until she sagged against him.

He stroked her back with one hand and showered kisses on her face and throat. "Katie, my love," he whispered. "I've missed you beyond belief. I couldn't think, couldn't work efficiently, couldn't sleep."

He leaned back to look at her. Perspiration dotted her forehead and her hair was a silky, disheveled tangle around her face. Her full lips were swollen and red and looked delectable to him and she had a half-lidded lethargic gaze that heated him in spite of his release.

"I've missed you," she said solemnly. "I'm glad you're home."

He leaned close to kiss her briefly and then pulled back. "I saw the table," he said. "Dare I hope we're celebrating my return?"

"Yes, plus a little bit more. Put me down and let me get on some clothes."

"You won't eat like you are now?"

"I certainly won't. Put me down."

"I'll put you down in the shower with me," he said, setting her on her feet and then scooping her back into his arms to carry her to a downstairs bathroom, where they showered together. She stepped out, grabbed a towel to dry swiftly, waving her hand at him. "Dry yourself," she said, throwing him a towel. "I want to go eat dinner."

Watching her, he thought he could look at her naked body forever. She was feminine, perfection in his eyes, all curves and soft and long legs and blond hair.

He placed his hands on his hips to focus totally on her and she paused, blushing.

"Get dry and stop staring at me."

"Look what you do to me so easily," he said. He was aroused, hard and wanting her again in spite of just making love.

"I'll get out of here and you step under cold water and cool down so we can eat. I have things to tell you."

He barely heard her, but he watched her wrap a towel around herself and rush out of the room. Even though he wanted to reach for her, he let her go. There would be later, after dinner. His stomach growled with hunger, but that wasn't the consuming hunger he ached to appease. He desired her again. He wanted to make love to her by the hour.

He stepped into the shower to take a brief, cold shower and see if it would cool him.

After drying, he wrapped a towel around his middle to go get his clothes. She met him in the doorway with his clothing in her hand.

"Looking for these?" she asked, holding them out.

"Thanks," he replied, trailing his fingers along her arm and hand before taking his clothes. "I'll be right there," he said. She nodded and left and he watched the slight sway of her hips as she walked away and he knew the cold shower had been useless.

Katherine went to the kitchen to put finishing touches on their dinner and to wait for him. She paused, thinking the moment was perfect because right now her career was skyrocketing and Cade was back in her life. It was all she could possibly want.

She knew it wouldn't last—not the part with Cade and that hurt and she decided to refuse to think about it as long as they were together. She couldn't wait to tell him her news and share her happiness with him.

"Here I am," he said, striding into the room in tan slacks and a dark brown shirt that heightened his tan. "What's got you so excited?"

"You, of course," she said smiling at him while he crossed the kitchen to open white wine she had chilled. "Plus a surprise that I wanted to tell you in person."

"There's something besides me that's making you glow? Could it be cold, hard cash?" he asked and she laughed.

"Don't be cynical! I have a surprise that I'll share with you," she said, kissing the corner of his mouth and wishing he would smile.

"Tell me now," he said with a dark premonition of disaster. "You're too excited. This is something big, isn't it?"

"Yes! It's big and it's partially because of you and I'm thrilled and gloriously happy."

He held her away from him to look at her. "You look radiant. I'm waiting, Katie," he declared solemnly, his foreboding increasing. "What's your big news?"

"Have you ever heard of the Chavin Corporation?" Katherine asked.

"Sure, old international manufacturing firm that has diversified in the last ten years and now is into various types of business. They own a chain of retail stores, hotels. They've moved some of their manufacturing overseas."

Cade crossed the room. "Let me pour glasses of wine, and then before we have dinner while we drink our wine, you can tell me," he said. "I'm sure they've made you an offer of some sort."

"You're right," she said, watching him open the bottle of white wine and pour two glasses. Carrying them as they walked to the sofa, he handed her a glass.

"Now tell me."

"You're right," she said, excitement bubbling in her. "They knew you'd hired me to paint these murals for you."

"How the hell did they know that?" he asked.

"They called my office and wanted to talk to me and the person they spoke to told them. I think it made a difference, Cade, because the first time they called, they were just making inquiries about my company."

"They called again?"

"Yes. Their vice president called me and I have an appointment to fly to their headquarters in Pennsylvania to talk to them about painting murals for their hotel chain. They indicated a large number of murals."

"Congratulations," he said quietly. "That's fantastic and evidently, just what you want."

"It won't interfere with the job I'm doing for you. I've already discussed that with them on a conference call. It would be after I finish this job." She grinned and took his wine from him to give him a hug.

"Thank you! If I hadn't done this work for you, I'm not sure they'd be as eager to hire me as they are. Between this job and that—if I get it—my future will be set!" she exclaimed, looking up at him as he swung her down to hold her in the crook of his arm. His dark gaze bore into her and she realized his expression was stormy, as a muscle worked in his jaw.

"What's wrong? You look angry, Cade," she said solemnly.

"We've gotten back together and twice now, I've had to return to California. I don't like it when I'm away from you, but it's bearable because I know I'll be here with you again. When I'm gone, I miss you, Katie."

She ran her fingers along his jaw, feeling the faint stubble of his beard. "I've missed you when you've been gone. Couldn't you tell?" she asked with a smile.

He didn't smile in return and she drew a sharp breath. She sat up and scooted off his lap to face him.

"I'd think you'd be happy. We've gotten together again—"

"Up to a certain point. Where are we going in our relationship?" He took her hands in his. His dark eyes blackened to midnight and the stormy expression deepened.

"I figured we were taking a day at a time," she answered solemnly.

"I love you," he said quietly, drawing his fingers along her cheek. Her heart pounded and a mixture of emotions rocked her. Magic words! Words that complicated her life! Words that she had yearned to hear. Words that were coming at the wrong time now.

"I love you, Cade," she replied solemnly. "I always have."

"I love you and I've always loved you," he repeated. "I want you to be my wife. Marry me, Katie."

Ten

Stunned, she couldn't breathe or move. "You've said you want family, a wife and children."

"Yes, I do," he answered evenly.

"I don't, Cade. I've made it clear to you that I don't. Or I thought I'd clarified my feelings. I'm on the brink of having an enormous expansion in my business and with your fee, I've already made more money than I ever dreamed about. Now, I'm set to put me on top in my business. I'll be able to take the jobs I want, command the pay I want—"

"I love you," he said, interrupting her and grinding out the words in a husky voice. He hauled her into his embrace, lifting her onto his lap again as he leaned over her to kiss her.

His tongue thrust deep into her mouth, and her protests vanished instantly. She moaned, winding her arms around his neck as he caressed her with one hand while he held her with the other arm and kissed her. Momentarily forgetting his anger, proposal or anything else, she clung to him, moving her hips with fires building again.

Abruptly, he stopped and looked at her. "Marry me. Love is a lot more important than career and money. Cash is damn cold comfort."

"Success is wonderful comfort!" she snapped. "That's so easy for you to say when you've done all this and you've made a fortune and you're a success beyond anyone's wildest dreams. You have it all! I want it! It's my turn, Cade!"

"I have the successful career and money, but I'd toss it if it meant I could have you."

"No!" she said. "You didn't toss it over nine years ago when you could have had me!"

"I left to protect my brother. I'd repeatedly turned down your father's offers of money until that time," he said. His eyes blazed and he kissed her again, silencing her protests, leaning over her and plunging his tongue into her mouth until she forgot their conversation and held him tightly. Her hips moved and she moaned.

As suddenly as before, he stopped. "You like being kissed, Katie. You like it a lot. You were meant for life and love and family and children."

"Don't tell me again what I'm meant for! I know what I want! I want my career, not marriage."

"You say one thing and then you do another. You respond to every touch, every kiss. You make love like it's the only time in your life you'll get to."

"Cade, I've gone into a relationship with you when I said I wouldn't. We're living here together, sleeping together. Why do you have to have marriage right now?"

"I want you forever," he said and her heart lurched.

"I can't do that."

"I want children with you. I want you to be the mother of my children because I think you'd be wonderful. I want my wife with me, though. I want a full-time wife who isn't sharing home life with a career."

"I don't want to do that," she said, rubbing her forehead.

"You're throwing a full life away with both hands," he said.

"If I say no to your proposal, does it mean you'll withdraw your offer about the murals?" she asked bluntly.

"No, you don't have to marry me to keep the damn mural job and get your millions!" he snapped while his face flushed.

"I just wanted to know where I stand with you," she said, getting up and breathing hard. His words hurt as much as a slap and anger shook her.

He stood and wrapped his arms around her waist. "I love you," he declared again. "I guess I've always loved you. After settling in California, I tried to forget you and thought I'd succeeded. When I returned to Texas, it was for the reasons I told you—to build my ego with the hometown folks, to hire the best mural painter, to have a connection to businesses in Houston and Texas. I wouldn't even let myself think about you except where business was concerned."

"So what happened that you do now?" she asked, looking up at him while her pulse drummed.

"You. When I saw you walk into the spotlight in that auction, I wanted you with a longing that I can't ever describe. I would have paid anything for the evening with you. And then when we were together, time and anger and hurt just fell away. The minute I kissed you, in some ways, we were back where we were nine years ago."

Drawing herself up and closing her eyes briefly, she placed her hands over her ears.

"Don't tell me those things! We're not back where we were nine years ago!" she cried, her eyes flying wide. She shook with hurt and anger. "I love you, Cade. I always have and I always will, but I love other things, too. I want a life you've achieved. You've been there and done that. I want my moment in the sun. I want success and my business to grow and the attention I'll get and the money I'll make. I want to flaunt it with my dad. Now, more than ever. Too many times he's made me feel small and incompetent."

"Dammit, grow up, Katie, and forget your dad. You don't have to prove a damn thing to him. He's still running your life if you do."

"Again, that's easy for you to say," she replied stiffly, angry with him and knowing they had an impossible chasm between them.

While they stared at each other, anger seethed and she could feel the clash of wills.

"I love you," he repeated quietly.

"I love you, too, Cade. But I know what I want and it isn't marriage, at least not on your terms." She walked away from him to look out the window without really seeing anything. She hurt and knew their relationship had changed again and the magic hours of lovemaking were over.

She heard his footsteps as he left the room and she turned to stare at the empty doorway.

She went back and sat on the sofa and picked up the wineglass to swirl the pale, amber liquid, watching it swish in the crystal glass. She hurt all over as if she had taken a bad fall. Everything ached and she knew he was angry and hurt, as well.

She swiped at tears. She wasn't going to cry over Cade again. She didn't want to marry and she had gone into a relationship with him when he'd sounded as if he would be satisfied to have that arrangement with her. Now he wanted marriage and with Cade it meant a full-time wife and it meant children.

She couldn't and she wished it didn't hurt so badly.

She heard his footsteps and looked up to see him with a briefcase in hand. "I'm leaving, Katie. You can have the place to yourself. When you want me to look at a mural, just let my office know and leave a message about what you want," he said.

Afraid if she answered him she might break into tears, she merely nodded.

He crossed the room to the door and then turned back to look at her. She gazed into his blazing dark eyes that burned with desire and suddenly he spun around.

Dropping the briefcase, he crossed the room in long strides to sweep her into his arms and kiss her, leaning over her. His mouth came down hard and his tongue thrust deeply into her mouth, stroking, plunging.

Unaware that salty tears spilled down her cheeks, she wrapped her arms around his neck and clung to him, kissing him back as wildly. Then she wanted him, wanting to kiss him and make love to him and give herself completely one more time.

Instead, he released her so abruptly she rocked on her heels and he was gone, striding away. He went through the door and slammed it shut behind him and in minutes she heard his car as he drove out of her life.

Hurting, she stood rooted to the spot for a few minutes until she put her head in her hands to cry.

Saturday morning she threw herself into work. The night had been sleepless and miserable, and today, the house was empty. She wanted to finish this job and get away from Houston.

Concentrating on her painting, she looked around when Mrs. Wilkson brought her the phone.

"You have a call," she said. Katherine's heart skipped a beat, as she hurriedly put down her brush and climbed down. To her disappointment, it was Matt, not Cade, and she listened to her brother.

"We want to get together with Laura—Mom. That seems weird to say when I haven't met her. Nick's in Europe, but I've talked to him and we thought we'd all fly to Houston next week to get together with you and her. We're aiming for Thursday night about seven and she'll have dinner catered. Bring Cade if you'd like. He's the reason this is happening."

"Sounds fine, Matt," she replied.

"You don't sound fine," he said.

"I'm fine. Really," she said.

"I can't believe it after all this time. We need to thank Cade. She sounds nice."

"She's wonderful," Katherine said.

"She can't wait to see Jeff. She's overjoyed to have a grandson that she's going to get to know."

"He's adorable and she'll love him," Katherine said and to her dismay, tears spilled over again.

"You're sure you're all right? You sound funny. Are you sick?"

"No. I'm fine. I'm working."

"Where's Cade?"

"He's gone back to California. He comes and he goes."

"All right. I'll let you know later what time we'll arrive. Katherine, I confronted Dad about it. It set him back and he's angry, but in time, I'm sure he'll adjust like he always does."

"Think he'll ever see her?"

"I can't predict that answer. It'll be good to see you, to this week," he added.

"Sure. You're a great brother," she said impetuously.

"Thanks. You're a great sister," he replied, and she ran her fingers over the phone as she broke the connection. She thought about her brother Matt and his concern. They would all soon be together. Her mother and her brothers and her baby nephew. Family. What Cade valued so highly.

Returning to work, she painted automatically while she thought about her brothers that she had always been competitive with because her father threw them up against each other and goaded them about one being better than the other. Why was she competing with Matt and Nick? They didn't compete with her, but they had vied with their dad and with each other over the years. They teased and tormented her at times when they were kids, but she knew it had been a big brothers and little sister thing. Since they had been grown, Matt and Nick never hesitated to show their fondness for her.

And why was she striving to best their father? What difference did it make? He was older and in frail health. Did she still crave his approval that badly?

She thought about Cade's advice to grow up.

You don't have to prove a damn thing to him. He's still running your life if you do. Remembering Cade's remarks, she knew he had been right. Was what she really wanted money and fame? Or had that become her substitute when Cade walked out and a way to get over the hurt?

Was she tossing away happiness? She thought about Nick and Matt, who, since their marriages, seemed happier than they had ever been in their lives. Little Jeff was precious and when she kept him, she missed him when they took him home.

She went back to work, her mind on her future and what she really wanted. What if she gave up her career?

She couldn't imagine doing such a thing. For the past nine years it had been the driving force in her life and she loved her work. How much did she love it? She had to ask herself.

She endured a sleepless night, struggling with losing Cade and facing a future without him.

She constantly reflected on her future. She could feel happiness slipping away, yet at the same time, she couldn't imagine getting out of business just when she was on the brink of having everything she had dreamed of and more besides.

Sunday morning gave her a quiet hour in church where she didn't hear anything that was said, but simply pondered her life. Halfway through the afternoon, she climbed down to take a break, get a cold drink and sit down. She stared at the phone. Cade had moved on and she knew he would.

On the other hand, she hurt more with every passing hour. She put her head in her hands and rubbed her forehead. Give it all up and marry Cade. She thought about what it would be like and raised her head to look at the mural.

She wouldn't have to stop painting, just stop working. It was the same thing in her mind. Yet she wasn't getting happier with her decision.

She wanted him back. Could she give up her business and be Cade's wife?

She returned to painting, working carefully while her thoughts churned over her future. The more she weighed the possibilities, the better it seemed to accept Cade's proposal. If she didn't, her life now would be about as good as it would get and today wasn't that great.

She missed dinner without realizing it, but she was on the verge of calling Cade and telling him she had changed her mind.

She kept telling herself to give it time, to be sure, because she would be tossing away all she had worked for, but she felt stronger as time passed with her decision to call him.

Finally, she stopped painting, and stood and stared into space. She knew she wanted him and marriage and she'd give up her career for him, and she knew she didn't have to wait days to be sure about her decision.

She climbed down and picked up the phone to call his cell number. Her heart raced and she felt as if a burden had lifted from her heart.

Her heart thudded when she heard his deep hello.

Eleven

"Cade, it's Katherine."

"It's good to hear your voice," he said. "I've missed you, darlin'."

Her heart thudded and she gripped the phone tightly. "I want to see you. I thought I'd fly to L.A. if you're going to be there. I think the soonest I can make arrangements is the weekend because Matt and Nick are coming this week and we're all going to see Laura."

"I don't think I'll be in L.A. this weekend," he said and her heart plummeted because chances were, that meant that he didn't want to see her. She couldn't imagine that Cade wouldn't be able to switch his appointments around.

"Cade, I want to talk to you," she said.

"Good, Katie. That's really great to hear because I want to talk to you, too. Why don't we talk now?"

"I didn't want to over the phone. It's better in person."

"I agree with that—" he said and she heard his voice clearly and in person. She spun around to see him standing in the doorway with his cell phone in his hand.

"Cade!" she shrieked and dropped the phone. Ignoring the clatter of the phone, she dashed across the room without thinking.

He stepped inside, closed the dining room doors and caught her when she threw her arms around his neck.

"You're here!" she said, covering his mouth with hers before he could answer. He held her tightly against him. Her feet weren't touching the floor, but she didn't care while they kissed passionately, her heart thudding that he was here in her arms, holding her, kissing her.

"I missed you," she cried and then kissed him again.

"Hey," he said, leaning back to look at her. "Don't cry," he said gently, wiping her eyes with his thumb. "Why're you crying, darlin'?"

He picked her up and carried her to a chair covered by a drop cloth where he sat and placed her on his lap. "Don't cry, Katie. There's no need for tears."

"I love you," she whispered, stroking his face. "I want to marry you, Cade."

His eyes darkened and he inhaled deeply. He bent his head to kiss her again, a kiss that scorched her and turned her toes and made her want him desperately. And convinced her she was making the right decision.

"Ah, Katie, you'll make me the happiest man on this earth." He framed her face with his hands. "Why the change of heart?" he asked, studying her.

"I was miserable without you," she said. "I thought about what you said about competing with Matt and Nick. That's foolish. They're not competing with me. Not that I'm any competition for them," she added.

"You are now, but your brothers love you and they're not

trying to keep you down or throw in your face that they make more money than you—which they may not any longer."

He gazed at her solemnly. "It was pure hell without you, Katie."

"Oh, Cade! My life is empty without you. And I thought about Matt and Olivia and Jeff—how happy they are. You're right."

"You think so? You're agreeing with me? You'll marry me?" he asked.

"Yes! Oh, yes!" she said, her pulse racing. She ran her hands over his shoulders and up to wind her fingers in his hair.

"What about a family, Katie? That's something that you have to want, not because I do, but because you do."

"I love my family and always have and we're together when we can be. You're right, Cade. That's all more important."

He pulled her to him to kiss her again hard, a kiss that reaffirmed their need and love. Her heart pounded with joy as she held him. Finally, he leaned away to look down at her.

"I've been thinking about us and the future, too."

"Is that why you came back here?" she asked, and he nodded.

"I'm glad you did—"

"Katie, I told you I didn't want my wife to work. I wanted my wife with me. I've thought about that and I guess I was unreasonable. You have a right to your life and your painting—that would be a crime when you're so talented if you gave up your painting. I can deal with it if you just don't have to have an international business or accept jobs that take you away from me for long periods of time. Can we compromise on that?"

She laughed. "I can compromise on anything! I let go of that drive, Cade. Dad's the one that shoved me into it. I don't need to work like I'm starving or have to own the biggest ad company or the most famous or anything."

He let out his breath. "That's the best news I've heard in

years," he said. "You're sure?" he asked, gazing at her solemnly with his probing, dark gaze.

"I'm very sure."

"I don't want you to wake up one morning and accuse me of taking your life away from you."

"No danger of that happening," she purred. "Not as long as you make love to me constantly and give me babies—"

"This is a big turnaround for you. Have you thought this through—?"

"Yes," she said, sobering. "I have. When you left, I hurt badly. Both times. I don't want to go through the rest of my life without you. The nine years have been dreadful enough. My work filled that void, but it was an emptiness in my life and in my heart."

"Oh, Katie, love!" he said, kissing her again, another long, hot kiss that set her pulse drumming.

When he paused, he said, "Wait a minute—" He tried to get to his trouser pocket beneath her bottom.

She wriggled. "What're you doing?" she drawled, rolling her eyes at him.

"Lean over," he said.

"Oh, my!" she gasped playfully and he grinned. He pulled a velvet box out of his pocket.

"Come back here," he said and handed her the box.

Surprised, she looked at the box and at him. She opened it to see a dazzling diamond. "Cade, it's beautiful!"

"Will you marry me?" he asked again.

"Oh, yes! Yes, yes!" she exclaimed, gloriously happy as he slipped the ring on her finger and then drew her back into his embrace to kiss her.

Two hours later in his big bed she waved her hand in front of them as she lay in the crook of his arm. "We're all getting together with Laura—Mom—Thursday night. We can announce our engagement then."

"Will it detract from your brothers meeting her for the first time?" Cade asked.

"I don't think so. We'll wait until later in the evening when things have settled."

"Sounds good to me."

"They want you to come anyway. I think Matt and Nick both want to thank you for looking her up."

"I'm glad I did. I told you that I debated about it and about telling you." He turned on his side and raised up, propping his head on his hand to look at her. "How soon can we marry?"

She thought about it. "We could just run away and do this and not have all that aggravation we went through before."

"It's whatever you want," he said drawing his finger lightly over the curve of her breasts just above the sheet that she had tucked beneath her arms. "You were sort of left standing at the altar, so to speak, last time. If it makes you feel better, we can have the biggest, showiest wedding ever. My family will all want to come."

She laughed. "All right. My family will want to be there— I don't know about Dad. He's going to be angry that you and I are marrying."

"We can carry on without him if we have to."

She thought about it. "Big wedding it is."

"I have the money so you can do whatever you want."

"So do I," she said, grinning at him.

"Then between us, pay people and get it done as soon as possible."

"Let's get a calendar," she said, sitting up. He stepped out of bed and crossed the room and her gaze raked over his muscled, naked body. "You are one good-looking man," she drawled when he returned and he grinned.

"You keep that up and you'll get me up."

"It's just talk," she said. "You're the best kisser, the sexiest man on earth—"

He rolled her over, moved on top of her to kiss her and the calendar fell to the floor until an hour later when they returned from the shower and she snatched it up to study it. She sat cross-legged and naked on the bed with the sheet tucked around her and beneath her arms. Cade lay beside her and drew his fingers over her back.

"This is almost the end of October. If you want it soon— how about a Christmas wedding?"

"Entirely too far in the future. We can have it sooner than that."

She studied the calendar. "Thanksgiving weekend? That's really soon."

"Too far away," he repeated. "Give me at least the week before Thanksgiving."

"Impossible!" she argued, remembering how quickly Nick and Julia planned their wedding. "Thanksgiving weekend is the soonest we possibly can."

He grinned. "You win since you're the bride and the main part of the wedding."

"I believe you have an equal part."

"Not at all. People won't even know I'm there."

"All the women will," she said, wrinkling her nose at him. He pulled her down in his arms. "Thanksgiving it is."

Epilogue

With a fanfare of trumpets Katherine started up the aisle while her gaze was on Cade, who was breathtakingly handsome in his black tux. Her arm was linked through her father's. Olivia, Julia and five of Katherine's friends were bridesmaids, all smiling at her. She barely glanced at them because she couldn't look away from Cade.

Her father placed her hand in Cade's and together she and Cade turned to the minister. Her heart pounded with joy and she looked into Cade's dark eyes as they repeated vows.

Losing all sense of time and forgetting the guests, she saw only Cade, thrilling as he declared his vows in his familiar deep voice.

Finally, they were pronounced man and wife and introduced to the guests. Cade linked her arm in his, and with trumpets and organ and violins playing, she walked back down the aisle as Mrs. Cade Logan.

In a blur they posed for pictures, Olivia and Julia helping straighten her white satin cathedral train.

"You're gorgeous," Cade said, leaning down to whisper to her before the photographer had them pose for the first picture.

"Let's have all the Ransomes together please. Husbands, wives, babies. Let's have a family picture," the slender photographer said.

"Well, here's the test for your dad," Cade said. "He almost didn't walk you up the aisle because of Laura. Now, will he get in the family picture if she does?"

"I don't know, but we all wanted her to join us, and she promised us she would pose with us," Katherine said, holding Cade's hand. She didn't want to stop touching him, longing to be alone with him, but she knew they had hours to go yet.

Laura, in a pale blue silk dress, stepped to one side of Nick's wife, Julia. Katherine saw her father standing off to one side of the room. "Dad?" Katherine called.

He clamped his lips together and went to stand beside her, crowding in between Katherine and Matt, who stepped aside to make room.

They posed and she wondered if he had even spoken to Laura, or Laura to him, but Katherine couldn't worry about her father on her wedding day. The minute the family pictures were over, the older Ransomes disappeared from the group.

After the pictures Katherine and Cade rode in his limousine to the country club for the reception that was already in full swing with tables laden with food, flowers lining the walls and the musicians playing.

When Cade claimed her for the first dance, she had already unfastened the long train and she stepped into his arms in the slim, white satin dress that had a straight skirt.

"I want you all to myself," he said, his warm brown eyes devouring her.

Feeling giddy, she smiled up at him. "My sentiments exactly."

"So how soon can we get out of here?" he asked.

"Hours from now," she replied as they danced together in unison. "We cut the cake, we talk to everyone, we mingle—"

He glanced beyond her. "Do you really think anyone would miss us?"

She laughed. "Yes! And I'm not doing that on my big day. Finally, Mr. Logan, you're hooked! It took me ten long years counting from the time we started seeing each other. You're mine now and I want the world to know it!"

He grinned. "And you're mine," he said, his voice dropping as he leaned close to her ear. "And I want you to know it in bed tonight. I want to kiss every delectable inch of you."

She slanted him a heated look. "Whatever you get to do, I get to do it, too."

He groaned. "Now you're tormenting me. I'm going to set the clocks faster."

"It won't work, so forget it."

"Here comes your brother for a dance with you." The music ended as Matt stepped up to claim her for the next dance.

He smiled down at her and she gazed at her oldest brother fondly. "I thanked Cade again for going to see Laura. He's a smart guy, Katherine."

"I think so."

Matt smiled at her. "I hope you both have as much happiness as Olivia and I've found."

"Thanks," she said.

"I'm glad, too, you married and you're cutting back to working part-time. You've got people who can run the agency for you."

"I know I do. I'll see how it goes. I may cut back more later."

"Dad's in the corner in a grump."

"Will he ever speak to Laura?"

Matt shrugged. "I don't know. I'd say he hurt himself all

those years, too. She seems great. I don't like to think how he deprived us."

"No, don't because we can't undo the past. Our dad isn't the easiest person."

"Amen to that one," Matt said. "Here comes brother Nick to dance with you. I'm glad for you and Cade."

"Thanks, Matt," she said, turning to her other brother to dance with him.

"You look radiant today, my very beautiful little sister. Don't you let Cade whisk you off to California."

She smiled. "He won't all the time. Maybe some, but you two can come see us."

"His family is nice. They're friendly people. I remember one of his brothers from when they lived here before. I didn't know the others."

"Dad is giving them a wide berth, but they don't care and neither does Cade."

Nick smiled at her. "I hope you're very happy with Cade. Marriage can be paradise."

"I'm glad, Nick. You and Matt are happily married and you both deserve it."

"I don't know about deserving it, but we're happy and it's great. Here comes your new hubby. I guess he couldn't stay away through two whole dances." Nick released her hand and placed it in Cade's. "Here's my sister. Take care of her."

"I intend to," Cade said easily, looking at her and taking her into his arms. "Tell me again how long before we can go?"

"About ten minutes shorter than the last time I told you," she said. "Are you going to pester me with that all afternoon?"

"Probably until I get my way. If we have to mingle, let's begin," he said, taking her hand to go talk to guests.

Within a few minutes they were separated. Later, she was with him to cut the cake and then people clustered to talk to them and she was separated from Cade again until shadows grew longer across the club lawn.

Cade appeared at her side. "Now?" he asked, tapping his watch.

"What a pest!" They both laughed, and she nodded. "Now."

"C'mon. Just go change and no goodbyes. Instead, you can say hello when we get back," he said, taking her hand and leaving with her to climb into the limousine and drive to the business airport, where he had his private jet waiting.

Within hours they were in a villa on an island in the Caribbean where their bedroom opened to the beach. She stepped outside and inhaled. "It's gorgeous and it smells wonderful!"

"I agree absolutely," he said in a husky voice, coming to stand behind her. "We have this island to ourselves for the next two weeks. This place is stocked with food. On Saturday, a crew comes to clean and restock, and we can swim and laze on the beach and stay out of their way. Otherwise, it's just us."

She turned to wind her arms around his neck. "This is wonderful, Cade."

"It is. See, I told you I'd get my money's worth that night I bid for an evening with you."

She wrinkled her nose at him. "I'm glad you bid and got the evening with me. I'm glad you came back."

"Your father didn't speak to me today. All he did was glare at me."

"I suspect it's more for bringing Laura into our lives than for marrying me. Either way, he'll start speaking to you when you give him a grandchild. That's the way he was with Olivia and now you saw how he dotes on her."

"Well, for the time being I want you all to myself before we start on this presenting him with a grandchild business."

"I'm not getting younger. My biological clock is ticking."

"You've got a little time left, old girl. Give me a few months before we start on a baby."

"A few months of spoiling you and loving you and giving you all my attention," she said, showering him with kisses between each word while her hands moved over him, pushing away his tux coat that fell in a heap. He stepped out of his shoes while he kissed her and his hands went behind her to unzip the pale blue silk dress that he pushed off her shoulders.

Her dress fell around her ankles while she unfastened the studs on his shirt and pushed open his shirt. His arms slid around her and he pulled her tight against him.

"I love you, Katie. I've always loved you."

"You're the only man in my life, Cade," she answered solemnly. "You're the only one I've truly loved ever," she said. "I've waited to be Mrs. Cade Logan a long time and we have nine years of loving to make up for."

"And we're starting now," he replied. He kissed her, his mouth coming down hard on hers.

She wound her arms around his neck and stood on tiptoe, kissing him in return, moving closer against him while she held him. "Cade," she whispered, raising her head. "I love you."

"I feel like I've waited forever to marry you," he said. "You're mine, now, Katie. Now and forever."

She closed her eyes and kissed him again. Happiness filled her and she knew he was the only man for her for all time.

* * * * *

New York Times *bestselling author*
Linda Lael Miller
is back with a new romance
featuring the heartwarming McKettrick family
from Silhouette Special Edition.

SIERRA'S HOMECOMING
by Linda Lael Miller

On sale December 2006,
wherever books are sold.

Turn the page for a sneak preview!

Soft, smoky music poured into the room.

The next thing she knew, Sierra was in Travis's arms, close against that chest she'd admired earlier, and they were slow dancing.

Why didn't she pull away?

"Relax," he said. His breath was warm in her hair.

She giggled, more nervous than amused. What was the matter with her? She was attracted to Travis, had been from the first, and he was clearly attracted to her. They were both adults. Why not enjoy a little slow dancing in a ranch-house kitchen?

Because slow dancing led to other things. She took a step back and felt the counter flush against her lower back. Travis naturally came with her, since they were holding hands and he had one arm around her waist.

Simple physics.

Then he kissed her.

Physics again—this time, not so simple.

"Yikes," she said, when their mouths parted.

He grinned. "Nobody's ever said that after I kissed them."

She felt the heat and substance of his body pressed against hers. "It's going to happen, isn't it?" she heard herself whisper.

"Yep," Travis answered.

"But not tonight," Sierra said on a sigh.

"Probably not," Travis agreed.

"When, then?"

He chuckled, gave her a slow, nibbling kiss. "Tomorrow morning," he said. "After you drop Liam off at school."

"Isn't that…a little…soon?"

"Not soon enough," Travis answered, his voice husky. "Not nearly soon enough."

Harlequin® Historical
Historical Romantic Adventure!

Loyalty...or love?

LORD GREVILLE'S CAPTIVE
Nicola Cornick

He had previously come to Grafton
Manor to be betrothed to the beautiful
Lady Anne—but that promise was broken
with the onset of the English Civil War.
Now Lord Greville has returned as an
enemy, besieging the manor and holding
its lady prisoner.

His devotion to his cause is swayed by
his desire for Anne—he will have the
lady, and her heart.

Yet Anne has a secret that must be kept
from him at all costs....

On sale December 2006.
Available wherever Harlequin books are sold.

REQUEST YOUR FREE BOOKS!

2 FREE NOVELS PLUS 2 FREE GIFTS!

Silhouette® Desire®

Passionate, Powerful, Provocative!

SDES06

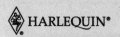

HARLEQUIN®

American ROMANCE®

IS PROUD TO PRESENT

COWBOY VET
by Pamela Britton

Jessie Monroe is the last person on earth
Rand Sheppard wants to rely on, but he needs
a veterinary technician—yesterday—and she's the
only one for hire. It turns out the woman who
destroyed his cousin's life isn't who Rand thought
she was. And now she's all he can think about!

"Pamela Britton writes the kind of
wonderfully romantic, sexy, witty romance
that readers dream of discovering
when they go into a bookstore."

—*New York Times* bestselling author
Jayne Ann Krentz

Cowboy Vet *is available from*
Harlequin American Romance in December 2006.

www.eHarlequin.com   HARPBDEC

Silhouette®

Desire